Diamond Spirit

1

DIAMOND
SPIRIT

Diamond Spirit

KAREN WOOD

ALLEN&UNWIN

First published in 2011

Allen & Unwin
83 Alexander Street
Crows Nest NSW 2065
Australia
Phone: (61 2) 8425 0100
Fax: (61 2) 9906 2218
Email: info@allenandunwin.com
Web: www.allenandunwin.com

Cataloguing-in-Publication details are available from the
National Library of Australia www.trove.nla.gov.au

ISBN 978 1 74237 315 7

Cover photo by Pip Blackwood / Wildlight
Cover and text design by Ruth Grüner
Set in 11.3 pt Apollo MT by Ruth Grüner
This book was printed in February 2014 at McPherson's Printing Group,
76 Nelson St, Maryborough, Victoria 3465, Australia
www.mcphersonsprinting.com.au

9 10

*For Shara Alisye, Jessica Tara, Jessica Rose
and Jody Grace.
You'll always have a place in my heart.*

1

'HEY, DIMEY, you're going on a holiday!'

Jess ran a soft brush over Diamond's sides, making her gleam. The pony was a picture of health. 'You and Rocko together, eating yourselves stupid for three whole weeks!' Jess swapped the brush for a comb and began untangling Diamond's thick black tail. Speckles and dots blanketed the pony's Appaloosa rump and three distinct silver diamonds trickled down her hindquarters like falling stars.

Her phone buzzed and rumbled in her jeans' pocket.

Shara: S^

Jess grinned and looked to the top of the driveway, where Shara stood waiting. She gave the tail a few more quick strokes and then pulled the pony's lead rope from the fence.

Shara was her buddy, her bestie, and the two of

them had just finished a brilliant season at pony club, competing as pairs in mounted games. They had spent every weekend vaulting on and off their horses, stabbing balloons, diving through hula hoops and shuffling in sack races while their ponies cantered along behind them. They'd had heaps of fun and won a stash of ribbons and trophies, including second place at the state championships, and now their ponies would be having a well-deserved break down on the grassy river flats.

Jess leapt effortlessly onto Diamond and trotted her bareback up the driveway. The little pony whinnied as they made their way out onto the road. Not far away, a horse answered with a long, throaty call.

'Coo–ee!' Shara waved as she appeared around a bend on Rocko, her chunky chocolate-brown quarter horse: a total basket case she'd bought cheap from the saleyards. She wore shorts and her old black helmet with horse stickers all over it. Her thick, straw-blonde pigtails poked out either side of her moon-shaped face. Hex, her part dingo, and Petunia, her half-blind cattle dog, followed. Shara's animals were a motley lot of stinky, bad-mannered rejects, but she adored all of them. They went everywhere with her.

'Ready for a holiday, Diamond?' Shara said, leaning over and giving the pony a rub on her golden neck. 'Packed your teeny weeny bikini?'

'And her sunnies and fake tan,' Jess laughed. 'I'm going to go crazy not riding for three weeks. Don't know what I'm going to do with myself.'

'Same!' said Shara.

They left the road and made their way down a grassy easement that ran between two properties, following a well-worn track to the first of many river crossings. The Coachwood River ran through the valley like a long, snaking highway, flanked with flat green pasture. The river flats had no permanent fences, but farmers often grazed their stock on the lush pasture using temporary electric ones.

'I was thinking we should spend the next three weeks building a cross-country course down here,' said Shara. 'Dad could use the tractor to drag some logs out of the river.'

'That'd be cool,' said Jess, her eyes lighting up. 'There are heaps more over by the sawmill. We could pile them up and make jumps out of them. No one would care.'

'And I'm going to have a huge clean-up – my tackroom, all my gear, the feed shed,' said Shara. 'I'm going to get it all ready for the holidays.' She ducked as she rode Rocko into the trees that ran alongside the river.

'Same,' groaned Jess. Her shed looked like ground zero. She would need to hire a bulldozer and a disaster response team to get it sorted out.

'I might have to do some swotting, too,' said Shara in a *just-letting-you-know* voice. 'I'm going to apply for Canningdale College.'

'Apply for *what*?' asked Jess.

'Canningdale – it's the only school in Australia that does animal science in Year Ten.'

'Never heard of it,' said Jess, frowning. 'Where is it?'

'New South Wales.' Shara gave Rocko a kick and pointed him straight down into a shallow crossing in the river.

'*New South Wales?*' said Jess. 'What do you want to go there for? It's full of cockroaches!' She let Diamond stop beside Rocko to have a drink from the cool clear water.

Shara smiled. 'It's where all up-and-coming vets go, Jessy!'

'And it's freezing!'

'So knit me some socks.'

'But it's so far away,' said Jess, getting to the real point. 'What would you do, go and live there?'

'I'd board at the school and come home in the holidays.'

'*What?*' Jess squeaked. 'Move away?'

'Hang on, I have to get a scholarship first,' said Shara. 'It's all just an idea at the moment.'

'Would you come home for weekends?'

'No, too far.' Shara gathered her reins as Rocko brought his nose up from the water.

'So, no mounted games?' It was almost unthinkable. 'No riding?'

'I'd take Rocko with me. It's an agricultural school.'

Jess was speechless. Until now, mounted games had been Jess's and Shara's whole lives. It was all they ever talked about, all they ever thought about, all they ever *did*. She'd just assumed life would always be that way.

'Oh Jessy, don't look so crushed,' said Shara.

'I am. I mean, I'm not, I mean, I'm really excited for you, but'—Jess tried to laugh—'who will I hang out with at school?' It seemed such a stupid, selfish question. 'Who will I ride with?'

'I might not even get in, you know. The scholarships are really competitive; I'd have to be, like, in the top five per cent in the state or something. There's no way Mum and Dad could afford it otherwise.' Shara turned Rocko onto the open grassy flats. 'It's a long shot.'

Jess rode alongside, her brain whirling. Shara always came top of the class without really trying, but did that mean she was in the top five per cent of braininess in the whole of Queensland? 'You'd have to be some sort of freaky super-nerd,' she said.

'I would,' said Shara. 'Probably nothing to worry about.'

'You'd look good with a stethoscope around your neck, though,' said Jess, trying to make light of it.

'Reckon?' Shara giggled and held out her arms. 'I rather like the latex gloves, myself!'

'Right up to your armpits,' warned Jess.

Shara pushed Rocko closer to Diamond, and with a funny little reshuffle, hopped up onto her knees and then crouched like a frog on his back. She leapt sideways and landed behind Jess on Diamond. Then she wrapped her arms around Jess and gave her a squeeze. 'Gonna miss me?'

Jess elbowed her off, hopped up into a crouch herself, and jumped over and onto Rocko. It was the best way to mount him, she'd discovered. On the ground he often tried to bite or kick, but if you could bypass the teeth and heels, he was fantastic to ride. 'No, I won't have to,' she laughed and pushed Rocko into a canter. 'You're not that geeky!'

Before she knew it, Shara was galloping past her on Diamond, heels flapping. 'Race ya!'

'Watch she doesn't—'

She did. Diamond kicked her heels up into the air, and with nothing but a halter and rope to hold on to, Shara went sailing through the air and landed in the thick grass, squealing with laughter. Diamond skidded to a halt as she had been trained to do when her rider dismounted.

'—pigroot,' finished Jess, pulling Rocko up before he decided to join in the fun.

Shara stood and brushed herself off. 'Give me my horse back,' she demanded. 'This one's dangerous!'

Jess rode up next to Diamond and leapt back onto her. 'Not like your little angel.'

Shara took Rocko's rope and gave him a hug. 'He's just misunderstood, poor boy,' she said, as Rocko screwed his nose and bared his teeth at her. She pushed his sour face away and sprang onto his back.

They walked and talked and laughed, and all the while, Jess pushed aside a gnawing uneasiness in the pit of her stomach. Surely Shara wouldn't really leave Coachwood Crossing?

After a while they reached the pile of fencing gear. Then, with the horses tethered, they staked out the new paddocks and ran tape around the perimeter. Jess marked out a large square that crossed over a section of creek and had a few shade trees. She ran three strands of tape around the star pickets and pulled them good and tight, taking care the electric current wouldn't short out on any tall clumps of grass or overhanging branches. Shara put Rocko's paddock away from the riding trail so passing riders wouldn't be tempted to pat him.

When the paddocks looked like little horsey heavens, the girls released their ponies and watched them sniff around, roll gleefully in sand patches and then snatch greedily at the sweet green grass.

Seeing Diamond so happy brought a smile to Jess's face. 'You deserve it, girl,' she said. 'You're the best horse ever.' The little horse stared straight at Jess and cocked her head slightly to one side, her mouth full of grass. Her golden coat shone like liquid metal in the sun.

'*Second* best,' said Shara. 'Come on, race you to the creek. Let's have a swim!' She bounded off across the river flats, leaping over the long grass with her arms flapping madly.

Jess rolled her eyes, laughed and ran after her.

2

TWO WEEKS LATER, Jess sat in the sunroom out the back rubbing an oily rag over her saddle. It was Saturday, the big day – Shara was sitting her test. Jess had tried to be as supportive as possible and give her friend space when she needed to study. If she didn't get in, Jess didn't want to be blamed for distracting her.

In between swot sessions, they had built an amazing cross-country course. Jess just couldn't wait to get a saddle on Diamond and try it out. One especially tricky jump was like a ski ramp on the bank of the creek. They would jump it downhill and land in the water. Wicked!

Diamond was fat and happy down on the river flats; so happy, in fact, that she barely raised her head from the grass to say hello to Jess each day.

Bang, bang, bang.

Jess registered a noise from the front of the house. She glanced up at the line of trophies along the picture rail and the scores of ribbons hanging on the wall. Only one more week and she could ride again.

She dipped her rag into the oil, lifted the flap of the saddle and kept rubbing.

Bang, bang, bang.

Someone was knocking at the door. No one ever knocked around Coachwood Crossing. She heard voices: her father's and another man's.

'Jess!' called her father. 'You'd better come out here, love.'

'Hang on,' she called back. 'I'll just finish my saddle.'

'Jess, come *now*. It's Diamond.'

Jess dropped her rag and ran to the front door. 'Diamond?'

A man she had never seen before stood holding the flyscreen door open. Her father was pulling on his boots.

'Do you own an Appaloosa pony?' asked the man.

'Yes.'

'It's stuck in the cattle grid down near the old drovers' yards. I nearly ran over it.'

'My pony is about a kilometre up the river from there. It wouldn't be her.'

'Is it a buckskin Appaloosa with spots all over it?'

Jess's blood ran cold. She pushed past the man and grabbed her boots, then ran down the front steps after her father, who already had the car running.

'Why would Diamond be down near the drovers' yards?' she cried, as she jumped in. 'Her paddock isn't anywhere near there.'

'She must've got out,' said Craig.

'She was behind three strands of electric tape. I checked her this morning. It can't be her.' Jess's stomach churned. Cattle grids and horses were not a good mix.

'We'd better go and find out,' said Craig. 'Thanks, buddy,' he called out to the man, before ramming the ute into gear and accelerating up the driveway.

They sped along the dirt road until they reached an overgrown easement that ran between two properties and down to a small tributary of the river called Slaughtering Creek. Craig put the ute into four-wheel drive and let the bull bar push through chest-high weeds. Just before the line of trees that marked the river was an open gateway leading onto the old droving route that had once followed the river. Behind the gateway were some dilapidated cattle yards that hadn't been used for years.

'I can't see any horse,' said Jess, stepping out of the car.

'Well, there are no other cattle grids around,' said Craig.

Jess swore out loud. In the ditch next to the grid, Diamond lay with her head back, eyes blank. 'Oh my God, *Diamond*!' Jess squealed. She ran to the ditch.

Jess's eyes darted frantically over her pony's body and legs. Her stomach twisted when she saw the two front hooves jammed between the steel rails. She looked up desperately for her father. 'Dad, her legs are stuck. They're in the grid!'

Her dad knelt beside her, hand over mouth. He closed his eyes and swallowed.

'Dad,' Jess said, her voice starting to quaver. 'We've got to get her out. Her legs, Dad. Look at her legs!'

Diamond's legs were wedged tightly and bent at a weird angle.

'How are we going to get her out?' Jess looked urgently to her father for answers.

Craig took a deep breath. 'Okay, let's get it together, Jess,' he said, firmly. 'We won't be any use to her if we fall to pieces. Do you have your phone on you?"

Jess patted her empty back pocket and cursed again.

'Grab a halter from the car.' Craig took a step towards the pony and muttered something under his breath. 'And stop swearing.'

Jess ran to get the halter. She put it down beside her father and ran her hands over Diamond's neck. 'It's okay, we're going to get you out, Dimey. It's okay.' She took a large gulp of air and willed herself to keep it together. 'Hang in there. It'll be all right.'

'She must have really galloped through it. Her feet

have gone straight through the rails and her body's just kept going, I reckon.' Craig took hold of one of Diamond's feet. 'It's wedged in so tight!'

Diamond groaned.

'Don't hurt her,' sobbed Jess. 'Be gentle.'

'I'm trying to, honey, but we need to get her out of here. These rails'll cut off her circulation. Who knows how long she's already been in here?'

Another car rumbled through the easement. Craig looked over his shoulder. 'It's your mum.'

Caroline stepped out of the car in an old sarong and ugg boots. 'I ran into some strange man in our driveway. He said that—' She looked down and saw Diamond lying in the ditch. 'Oh crikey, Diamond. What have you done to yourself?'

'Caroline, can you race back to the house and ring the vet? Then hook up the horse float and bring it back.' Craig turned to Jess. 'Get that halter on her head, while I try to get her legs out.' He continued to push at the pony's legs.

Jess lifted Diamond's head and slipped the halter over her nose. She stroked her neck. 'It's okay, beautiful girl. I'm here. We're going to get you out,' she whispered as she buckled it along the pony's jaw with trembling hands. Diamond's eyes rolled to the back of her head. 'She's not moving, Dad. Why isn't she moving?'

'She's probably in shock,' said Craig, still working at the pony's legs.

'Why don't we cut the bars?'

'Do you know what it would take to cut through steel that thick?'

Behind him, the car door slammed and Caroline's car engine started up again.

'Bring some bandages back too,' called Craig.

'Okay,' said Caroline, as she pulled away and roared back towards the house.

'That's it. I've got one out,' said Craig, giving a final push. Blood spurted from the front of Diamond's leg as it squeezed out between the rusty steel.

'You've cut her!' squealed Jess. 'You've split her leg in half!'

'It's the only way I can get her out,' said Craig. 'Flesh can be healed, Jessy, bones can't. It's better than leaving all her weight hanging on those legs while they're twisted like that.' He took a breath and shoved the other leg out from the bars.

Jess stared in shock at Diamond's two front legs, slit right along almost to the bone. She felt sick. 'Dimey?' she whispered, but the pony was motionless, her head stretched back. 'Diamond, we got you out. It's okay, you're free.'

But the pony still didn't move.

'We should get her up,' said Craig, reaching for the lead rope.

'No, you'll hurt her,' said Jess. She snatched at the rope. 'Daddy, no.'

Craig pulled at the pony's head. 'She has to, honey. It's for her own good.'

'Please don't,' sobbed Jess. 'She can't, leave her alone!' She pulled at the rope.

Her father ignored her. 'Come on, girl.'

'Dad, stop it!' screamed Jess.

Her dad kept pulling until Diamond gave a mighty heave and struggled to her feet. Jess jumped back out of the way.

The pony stood squarely on all four legs, her head low. Both Jess and her father were quiet.

'It's okay, honey, she's up,' said Craig. He put his arms around Jess. 'She's going to be okay, she can stand.'

Jess shrugged him off. She threw her arms around Diamond's neck and sobbed. 'Thank God you're all right.'

3

IT WAS TWO whole hours before John Duggin, short and stocky in dark blue coveralls, stepped out of his car and gave Jess a warm smile. 'Sorry I couldn't get here sooner, Jess. A horse went down on the racetrack.' He lifted the back hatch of his car. 'What's happened?'

Jess told him as much as she could about the accident while he squatted down and began examining Diamond's legs. He ran a gentle hand over one fetlock and pressed gently with his thumb around the cut. With a small bucket of water and disinfectant, he began cleaning the wound and inspecting inside it. He tried to lift one of her legs but Diamond reared in protest.

Jess was relieved when he gave up. She gave Diamond a reassuring rub on the forehead while John went to his car and rummaged in the back. He resurfaced holding a needle and syringe. 'Let's make her more comfortable first.'

After a short while the pain in Diamond's eyes subsided and John was able to have another go at lifting her legs. He moved them about gently, squeezed, prodded and frowned without saying anything, then stood there with his hands on his hips, staring at the wounds. Jess watched his face. Something about his expression made her feel cold.

What? What are you thinking? Say something.

John scratched his chin. 'I think we should take some X-rays.'

It seemed to take hours to get Diamond's legs X-rayed, and for John to stitch her leg wounds and carefully wrap them in wads of cotton wool and bandages. As he lifted the heavy X-ray machine back into the car, he promised to let Jess know the results as soon as he could.

Jess led Diamond one slow, painful step at a time back to her yard and put her in the stall with a large haynet.

Half an hour later, Jess stared at Diamond. The pony stared at the wall. The haynet hung from its hook, untouched. Jess ran a hand along Diamond's back and over her speckled rump, tracing around the three silver diamonds as she often did. She knew every mark, every spot. She pulled her phone out of her back pocket.

It vibrated in her hand as though it had read her mind.

Shara: S^

Jess let herself out of the stall and ran to the front yard. Sure enough, Shara was stepping out of her mother's car. She skipped down the driveway, yelling, 'Guess what! Guess what!' before Jess could tell her about Diamond.

'What?'

Shara stopped, did a big star jump, and screamed, '*I made the shortlist for Canningdale!*'

'Oh my God,' said Jess.

'I have to do the final test on Wednesday. It's a maths test!' Shara jiggled up and down on the spot.

Shara was a total brainiac at maths. She got a hundred per cent every time. How could anyone beat that? If selection got down to maths, Shara was in. She'd be leaving in a matter of weeks, at the end of the school holidays. Jess blinked back tears.

'Jessy, don't,' said Shara.

'Don't what?' said Jess.

'Get all emotional.'

'I'm not,' said Jess, bursting into sobs.

'You are.' Shara put her arms around Jess. 'Stop it. You'll make me cry too!'

'Sorry,' sniffed Jess, squeezing Shara tightly. 'I can't help it.'

Shara winced and shrunk away from her. 'Ouch.'

'What?'

'Nothing,' said Shara quickly. 'Come on now, this is over the top. We'll still ride together in the holidays. We'd probably start having different classes next year anyway.'

'Sorry. I'm really happy for you,' said Jess. 'You'll be a vet . . . with a stethoscope and long latex gloves.' She wiped at her eyes and tried to laugh. 'But you're leaving me, and Diamond's hurt, and I think she's going to die.'

'What?' Shara's face dropped. 'When? Where? What are you talking about?'

Jess led her to the stable and told her everything. Shara was unusually quiet as Jess ran her finger over the front of Diamond's bandages, showing where the cuts were. 'I don't know how she got down there. She was miles from her paddock. And she must have been galloping. Why would she be galloping? Something must have been chasing her.'

Shara seemed dumbstruck. She stood staring at Diamond's bandages with a remote look on her face.

'How do you reckon she got out?' asked Jess.

'I don't know,' shrugged Shara.

They both stood there, staring at Diamond. The little horse, usually so full of cheek and personality, stood listlessly, her head low, eyes half shut.

'She'll be okay,' said Shara finally. 'Ponies are tough. Look, she's putting weight evenly on both legs. I've seen some pretty bad cuts and they always heal in the end. We can find you another horse to ride in the holidays.'

'I don't want to ride another horse,' said Jess. 'This isn't about riding. This is about Diamond. You should have seen how much pain she was in before John gave her a needle. She could hardly stand.'

Shara ran her hand along Diamond's neck. 'You'll be amazed at how quickly she heals, though. She'll be fine.'

'John took X-rays. He's going to ring me when he gets the results. Her legs might be—' It was all Jess could bring herself to say.

'He would have put her down straight away if her bones were broken. You're worrying about nothing, Jess.'

'I knew I shouldn't have put her down on the river flats,' Jess moaned. She heard Shara inhale and instantly regretted saying it. 'I know you thought it was a good idea, but . . .'

'How was I to know she'd push through the fence? Most horses don't do that.'

'Diamond doesn't push through fences.'

'I knew you'd think that.'

'Think what?' asked Jess. Why was Shara being so weird?

'Nothing.'

'Think *what*, Shara?'

'*Nothing*, I said. Don't worry about it.'

'I'm not blaming you,' said Jess. 'You're right; the hot-wire should have kept her in. I just can't understand how she got through three strands of electric fencing. It was all over the place, like something had galloped through it. The whole thing just doesn't make sense.'

'Maybe it was wild dogs. They hunt in packs.'

'A dog wouldn't pull an electric fence down.'

'Probably not,' agreed Shara. 'Listen, I gotta go. I have to study for that exam.'

'But you just got here!'

Shara looked uncomfortable. 'Sorry, I guess I'm a bit caught up about Canningdale. But I know she'll be all right. John's one of the best vets in the country. He'll fix her. We'll be riding again in no time.'

Jess forced a smile. 'Good luck on Wednesday!'

'Besties?'

'Besties.'

Shara had barely disappeared from the driveway when the phone in the shed rang. Jess raced to pick it up. 'Hello?'

'Jess.' John's voice was soft and gentle – more so than usual.

It's bad.

'What . . .' Tears welled up inside her. 'What did they show?'

'There are more than a dozen bone fragments chipped off her pastern joints. Her legs are buggered, Jess.'

Jess felt the air squeeze out of her lungs.

'We're going to have to make some tough decisions, matey.'

Jess breathed in and wiped at her eyes. 'I thought horses couldn't walk if they broke their legs.'

'She *can't* walk,' said John. 'Without painkillers, she can barely stand.'

'But . . . so what are we going to do?' Surely there was *something* he could do. This was Diamond they were talking about. Not some racehorse that had gone down on the track. She didn't care if she never rode Diamond again, she just wanted her fixed. She waited for John's answer.

He sighed heavily. 'I could try to save her. I could operate on her, but there'd be no guarantees. She would have to live on drugs for the rest of her life. That would give her stomach ulcers . . .' He trailed off.

'Will she ever stop being in pain?'

'I don't think so.'

Jess went mute as she struggled to comprehend.

'How about I go and have another look at the X-rays,' said John, 'and think about what sort of surgery might be possible. I'll come over—' he paused, as though flipping through a diary, '—and we'll sit down with your parents and have a proper talk about it. I have surgery on Monday and Tuesday, but I could come over on Wednesday.'

Jess stared at the shed wall, numb.

'How does that sound?'

She nodded and put down the phone.

4

WEDNESDAY CAME. Jess had already made her decision. She sat out in the paddock with her elbows on her knees, forcing herself to breathe evenly. The spring-time smells of freshly cut pasture and wattle flowers, mixed with horse, wafted up her nostrils and a tractor spluttered somewhere across the valley. She closed her eyes, savouring the warmth of the early-morning sun on her face. It seemed all wrong that it could be such a beautiful day.

Beside her, Diamond grazed on the soft new grass. *Rip, rip, chew* – it was a familiar sound that helped Jess feel calm. The pony nibbled closer and closer until she was snuffling at Jess's lap. She smiled and rubbed the pony's forehead. 'Diamond.' She put her face against the pony's cheek. 'I love you so much, little girl.'

She glanced at her watch: half an hour to go.

Diamond shifted her weight from one bandaged leg to

the other and closed her eyes to chew, as though she too just wanted to stay in this moment.

Caroline burst out of the flyscreen door, buttoning a threadbare flannelette shirt above her sarong. 'Crikey, Jess, John's here already!' she called. John Duggan's car rumbled down the dirt road and slowed before turning into the driveway.

Jess stood and put her arms around her pony's neck. She buried her face into Diamond's mane.

She heard a car door open and then slam.

I can't do this.

Footsteps.

A soft voice.

'You okay, matey?'

Jess pulled her head out of Diamond's mane and looked directly into John's eyes. They were kind and wise, and she trusted them. 'I'm doing the right thing, aren't I?' She had to be absolutely sure.

'Yes, I think it's the right thing, if you really care about her. She'll always be in pain, and that pain will only get worse.'

Jess nodded. A cold, sinking feeling pushed down on her, making her feel heavy and stiff.

John put a hand on her shoulder. 'What do you want to do? Would you like your mum to take you up to the house?'

'No, I want to stay.'

John glanced across at Caroline.

'She's okay,' said Caroline. 'We made this decision together, didn't we, Jess?'

Jess nodded and looked down at the ground. If she made eye contact with anyone right now, she would fall to pieces. She led Diamond slowly to the old coachwood tree at the top of the garden.

John stood with his feet apart and his hands behind his back. 'There are two needles,' he said. 'As soon as I give her the second one she'll be gone. It's very quick and she won't feel a thing. She'll be gone before she reaches the ground.' He paused. 'Okay?'

'Yep,' she whispered. Her heart slammed against her ribs.

'All right, here we go,' said John softly. 'Is this where you'd like her to rest?'

Jess nodded. Her heart felt as though it were trying to jump out of her body. She concentrated on breathing.

'Here we go, little one,' said John, giving Diamond a pat and then, with his hand cupped under the pony's neck, he pressed his thumb onto her jugular to distend the vein.

Jess's eyes froze on John's hand as he inserted a needle. Blood dripped onto the ground.

'It's okay; it's just a little blood. I'm putting the syringe on now.' John hooked the syringe onto the needle and pressed the plunger. Then he pulled the syringe off, hooked a second one on and injected the final dose. 'There we go, little girl,' he said, as he took the halter from Jess and eased Diamond to her knees and onto the soft earth.

'I love you, Diamond!' Jess cried, as her pony gave a last long exhalation, then lay motionless. Jess's knees buckled and she lay over Diamond's warm body, her face against the pony's neck. She could hear an eerie distant whine, like a helium balloon deflating across a room; it was coming from her own lungs.

'It's okay, darlin'.' Caroline knelt beside her. 'Breathe in and out slowly. You're hyperventilating. It's okay. She's out of pain now. We couldn't have her in pain.'

Jess concentrated on her breathing and began to feel calmer. A strange nothingness settled over her. 'Oh, Mum, she's really gone.'

She laid her cheek on Diamond's neck. It was so still.

5

JESS SAT AT THE kitchen table, chewing slowly on a cold piece of toast. She hadn't managed to pull herself out of bed until well after lunchtime. Normally she never slept in. She always fed Diamond, checked her water, took off her rugs and gave her a quick brush before she even had breakfast. But today wasn't a normal day. Diamond was dead and her parents had let her stay home from school. The rest of the day stretched blankly in front of her.

'Better feed Hetty's horse, I suppose,' she said to Caroline, pushing aside her plate and standing up. Her cousin's gelding had been trucked from drought country out west a couple of days before; Caroline had offered to take him in for a few months to save him from being sent to the saleyards.

'Don't you think you should put some shoes on?' Caroline called after her.

'No.'

Down at the shed she stuffed some hay into a net and tossed a dipper of pellets into a bucket, then carried it all out to the paddock. 'Hee–up!' she called. The gelding continued to graze. 'Oy, horse! Want a feed or what?'

The old stockhorse turned a slanty eye in her direction and kept eating. He was from the pebbly open downs of Longwood, where the pasture was sparse: buffel and button grasses mostly, flanked by mulga flats and spinifex ridges. Like most of the horses Jess had seen from out that way, he was ribby, with a dull, sun-bleached coat.

She rattled the pellets and finally the horse looked up and came towards her. He shoved his remarkably ugly head into the bucket, knocking it from her hand, and then began hoovering the pellets from the ground. 'Charming,' mumbled Jess.

She wandered to the coachwood tree. Its ancient trunk was circled with silvery rings, and the canopy was covered in squillions of creamy flowers shaped like stiff little stars. There were hundreds of these trees along the local creeks, but this was the biggest one Jess had ever seen. Somehow it seemed ancient and wise. Each November she loved to watch its flowers turn from cream to pink. The pinker they got, the closer Christmas was.

Next to it, Diamond's resting place was a mess, with tyre marks everywhere. The horror of the previous day confronted her: Diamond flopped in the hole with no life in her body, her eyes glazed blue and empty.

Jess sat down where she thought the pony's head would be. She pushed her face between her knees, stared at the ground and inhaled the smell of fresh soil. She pushed her toes into the cool earth, trying to feel close to Diamond, for what seemed like hours.

Buzz rumble.

Shara: S^

Jess turned and saw Shara standing at the top of the driveway holding a bunch of yellow flowers, the kind that grew along the railway line between their two homes.

'You didn't tell me that Diamond was going to be put down!' said Shara. She began walking towards Jess. 'I heard it from Katrina and Tegan this morning. How could you not tell me? I never would have gone to that test.'

Jess just stared at her.

'I can't believe it,' Shara said, gazing around at the mud. 'Is this where she's buried?'

Jess nodded. Shara sat down next to her and the two girls sat in silence for a while.

'How was the test?' asked Jess, with an effort.

'Easy. Who cares about the stupid test?'

'Why aren't you at school?'

'It's four o'clock, Jess. I can't believe you didn't tell me,' said Shara again. 'I didn't know, or I would have been here.'

'You would have blown your test.'

'I could have sat it later.'

'No, you couldn't.'

'Why didn't you at least tell me?'

Jess was quiet for a while, because she really didn't know the answer. Eventually she shrugged. 'I didn't want to. I only had such a short time left with her. Sorry, but I just couldn't share her.'

'Jessy . . .' Shara paused. 'Why don't we go for a ride?'

'What?' Jess turned and stared at her. 'You must be joking.'

'You could ride that bay horse.'

Jess screwed up her nose. 'What, Hetty's horse?'

'Yeah, why not?'

'I don't want to ride him. I can't even catch him!'

'Didn't you say he'd done pony club?' said Shara. 'How wild could he be?'

'He's about a hundred years old,' said Jess. 'He'll probably have a heart attack and drop dead on me.'

'Oh come on, Jess, he'll be all right.'

'I really don't feel like riding today. It's way too soon.'

'But it's impossible to be sad on the back of a horse,' said Shara. 'You say that all the time.'

'Well, maybe I want to be sad,' said Jess.

'Come on,' Shara pleaded. 'We'll just walk along the river flats and talk. That old fella will be fine. I promised Mum I'd exercise her new mare today.'

Jess shook her head. The last thing she felt like doing was jumping on someone else's geriatric horse. She couldn't believe that Shara had even suggested it.

'I'll run home now, saddle up and then come back and get you,' said Shara. She stood up to leave. 'Okay?'

'Oh, all right,' grumbled Jess. It couldn't be as bad as sitting around staring at an empty horse yard all day.

'Besties?'

Jess nodded. '*Best* besties.'

Jess rummaged through an old bag of tack and pulled out various bits and pieces. Diamond's gear wasn't going to fit that big clomper of a horse. After much sorting, buckling and rebuckling, she put together a sort-of-functional bridle and carried it out to the paddock.

The gelding stood with his back to her, resting a leg. When he saw her approaching, he screwed up his nose and walked away. Jess followed him, lunged and grabbed a chunk of his mane. She was relieved when he let her put the halter on.

Back at the hitching rail, Jess ran a critical eye over him. He had a long scrawny neck and a head like a besser block. His coat was dull and shaggy and his feet were like chipped old dinner plates. 'What an embarrassment,' she said out loud. 'Well, I guess you'll do for a trail-ride, old fella. I just hope you're not a lunatic.'

She heard the clatter of horseshoes on the road.

'Come on, Jessy. Get that brumby saddled up,' Shara called out as she rode into the driveway on her mother's new horse, a huge bay mare. She jumped off and gave the gelding a pat on the forehead. 'Oh, he's a total sweetie! What's his name?'

Jess screwed up her face. What was it with Shara and ugly animals? 'I think it's "Dodger".'

'He's cute.'

'I've seen better-looking roadkill,' Jess mumbled under her breath, as she tossed her saddle over Dodger's back and reached under his belly for the girth. It only just fitted. As she struggled to get it to the first hole, he began to shift around. 'Stand up,' she said, in a quiet but threatening tone.

'He looks a bit ticklish,' said Shara.

Jess yanked at the girth. Dodger put his ears back,

inhaled, and inflated his belly like a balloon, causing the girth strap to slip out of the buckle and fall away.

'Come on, Piggy,' Jess said, giving him a nudge in the ribs and reaching for the girth again.

Dodger inhaled, deeper this time. He leaned towards her.

'Look at him; he's got no manners at all,' she said, slapping him on the belly. 'Stop it!'

In reply, Dodger pushed harder until Jess found herself squeezed firmly against the hitching rail. 'Crikey!' she wheezed, trying to push him off. She could have sworn he eyeballed her foot. 'Don't you dare!' she growled, pushing at his shoulder.

Dodger's hoof came down on her foot with half a tonne of horse behind it, leaving her gasping in pain. She hurriedly pulled her hoof pick from her back pocket and dug it into his ribs. The old horse snorted and jumped away, making the saddle slide from his back and land with a thud on the concrete slab.

'Untie his rope,' said Shara. 'He's gonna pull back!'

'Whoa, Dodger!' yelled Jess.

Dodger rolled his eyes and gave a gigantic heave. Both his front legs lifted from the ground and paddled wildly in the air. He threw his weight at the rope, twisting and shaking, until it snapped and catapulted him backwards, sending up a cloud of dust. Dodger scrambled to his feet, exploded off his hind legs and fled to the bottom end of the paddock. He bucked and squealed in triumph.

'That went well,' said Shara.

'He's totally crazy!' said Jess.

Shara picked up the broken shred of rope still tethered to the fence. 'Maybe you shouldn't have tied him to a solid post.'

Jess sat down behind the hitching rail. 'How was I to know he's a total nutter?'

'He just hasn't been handled for a while. He needs a gentle hand,' Shara said.

'A gentle hand? Are you kidding?'

'You're so uptight. No wonder he's freaking out.'

'*Uptight?*' Jess couldn't believe her ears. 'Why don't you go and saddle him up, if you're so relaxed? See how *you* go with him!'

'Okay then, I will,' said Shara, tethering the mare to the hitching rail. 'I tell you what: if I can do it one-handed, will you still come for a ride?'

'No, I think I'll go and do some yoga so I'm not so *uptight*,' Jess hissed.

Shara giggled and walked away to get Dodger. She caught him easily and saddled him with one hand, chatting quietly to him all the while. Dodger looked like an old school pony in her hands. His ears flopped lazily to the sides of his head and his lower lip hung open, a thin stream of dribble hanging from his chin. Finally, Shara held out the reins to Jess.

Jess snatched them from her. 'Just walk until I get used to him.'

6

THEY HEADED OUT the driveway and walked along the road. Every three or four strides, Dodger snatched the reins. 'He's trying to rip my arms off,' whined Jess.

'Give him a long rein and see if that helps,' said Shara, kicking her feet out of the stirrups and waggling her legs around. 'Just relax a bit.'

Aargh! If she says that one more time . . .

They came to the open flats where the river wove through the valley. At the next crossing they stood and let the horses drink, while Shara's dogs rolled about in the sandy patches and lay on their bellies in the cool water, panting happily. Jess closed her eyes and let the trickling sounds of the river flow through her soul. For a brief moment Dodger stopped snatching, and she exhaled.

Shara's big mare raised her head and let out an anxious whinny, breaking the serenity. Dodger did the same, sniffing at the air and stepping backwards. He seemed suddenly nervous. Their call was answered, and from around a bend in the river came a brilliant white horse with a finely dished nose and a long curly tail. Her name was Chelpie, and her rider, wearing a white shirt and black helmet, was Katrina Pettilow.

'Settle down, Chelpie,' Katrina said in an annoyed voice, and turned to the girl riding behind her. 'Tegan, keep back a bit. You're making her nervous. I told you she gets hard to manage when we ride near the river.' She looked down at the horse's back legs. 'You've splashed mud on her!'

Jess groaned inwardly. Katrina made such a big deal about her horse being white. 'Not many horses are *truly* white, you know, most are really just *greys* that fade with *age*,' Katrina would tell people. Like anyone cared. Then she would crap on about the genetics of white horses, and why her horse was so special. And although both Shara and Jess agreed that there *was* something special about the horse, they also agreed that there was something *truly painful* about the rider.

Her shadow, Tegan Broadhead, was equally so, even though there was nothing special about her small brown pony. She worshipped the ground Katrina walked on, which only encouraged her to be even *more* painful. Together, they were excruciating.

'Hello,' said Katrina, without quite looking Jess in the eye.

'Hi,' Jess mumbled.

Shara pretended to be busy adjusting her horse's girth.

Great, she's going to leave me to do all the talking.

Katrina pulled Chelpie to a halt. 'Sorry to hear about your pony,' she said. 'What was its name again?'

'Diamond,' said Jess.

'Oh yeah, that's right, knew it was something like that.' She pointed her dressage whip at Dodger. 'Is that your new horse?'

Behind her, Tegan snorted.

Without warning, Dodger pinned his ears flat back and lunged at Chelpie, almost dislodging Jess from the saddle.

'No, it's not my new horse,' she said, pulling him sharply away. 'Stop it, Dodger!'

'It's got a *bad* temperament,' said Katrina. 'Has it been abused or something?'

'Where'd it come from?' asked Tegan, looking at Shara. 'Get another one from the dogger's yard?'

Shara gave her a mock smile and said nothing.

'He belongs to my cousin,' said Jess. 'There's a drought out west, in case you hadn't heard.' Jess felt Dodger's back tense beneath the saddle as he lifted his tail. She smirked.

Nice timing, Dodger.

She turned in time to see a large green poo ooze like toothpaste from his rear end, hit the water and swirl towards Chelpie's curly white tail and silvery hocks.

'Oh, *yuck*!' said Katrina. She raised her whip and brought it down sharply on the little mare's rump. Chelpie shot out of the water with a cranky swish of her tail, sending a spray of green all over Tegan.

Jess smiled sweetly. 'Must be the change in his diet,' she said with a shrug. 'Sorry.'

'That horse is a welfare case, Jessica Fairley!' Tegan said, wiping her face with her sleeve. 'Gross! It's probably full of worms.'

'You can talk,' said Jess. 'Why don't you get a bigger horse and give that poor thing a break?'

'Yeah, why don't we just toss it out onto the river flats and let other people's horses chase it through a cattle grid? Why don't we just let it snap its legs in half?' Katrina retorted. She yanked on Chelpie's mouth. 'Come on, Tegan, let's get out of here.'

Jess's mind scrambled. She growled at Dodger to stop his head-tossing and gave him a sharp kick in the ribs. 'What did she mean by that?' she said to Shara.

Shara rode up next to her. 'Who cares? She's a slaggy ho-bag.'

'What did she mean by *other people's horses*? What other horses?'

'How would I know, I wasn't there,' snapped Shara. 'She probably just made it up. God, she annoys me. Come on, let's go down near the sawmill and try out some of our new jumps.' She trotted off.

Jess followed. 'Shara, wait!'

Before she could catch up, Shara was cantering over a large open field.

Near where Slaughtering Creek met the Coachwood River, the grass grew long and wispy, brushing the bottom of the girls' boots and rustling in harmony with the distant hum of farm machinery and intermittent bird calls. But the seemingly tranquil setting belied the edgy feeling it gave Jess. It was very close to the old drover's yards and horrible images of Diamond's legs were leaping into her thoughts. She brought Dodger back to a walk and tried not to look in the direction of the cattle grid.

Jess saw a tall man heading their way, calling out to them. As he got closer, she realised it was Lawson Blake, a local farrier – and he was carrying a gun. 'Shara, wait up!' she called out.

Shara slowed to a walk.

'You kids get out of here,' Lawson yelled.

'You can't tell us to leave,' Shara retorted. 'This is Crown land.'

Jess pushed Dodger into a trot and caught up with her. 'Let's just go, Shars.'

'I'm fed up with people stirring up my cattle,' Lawson shouted, waving an arm at them. 'Move it, and take those bloody dogs with you or I'll shoot 'em.'

'We haven't been anywhere near your cattle,' said Shara. 'We're just riding through.'

'Well, you just keep on riding, and don't come back.'

Shara ignored him. 'Come on, Jessy. Let's do some jumps. He can't tell us what to do.' Before Jess could protest, Shara kicked her mare into a canter and pointed her towards a pile of logs.

Lawson spat on the ground, then raised his gun. 'I'm warning you,' he yelled.

Shara kept riding.

Lawson shook his head and then the sky exploded.

Dodger went to pieces. He spun on his hind legs and threw his head back, his huge skull smacking into Jess's face with a sickening crunch.

She fought to open her eyes as he began to spin on the spot. The tighter she held him, the more he turned in crazy, dizzying circles, around and around, tossing his head frantically. Jess screamed.

'Jess!'

She couldn't tell where Shara's voice came from. It was like being stuck on the worst ride at an amusement park with the lights turned out.

'I'm coming, Jessy. I'm coming.'

The reins were pulled from her hands. 'Let go of his head, Jess. I've got him. Let go.' A hand grabbed her arm. 'Jump off! I can't hold him much longer.'

Jess let herself collapse off the horse. Dodger broke free and she listened to the fading drum of his hooves as he bolted into the distance.

She spat a glob of blood from her mouth and tried to get her breath back. Her face burned with a vicious heat and when she opened her eyes, she could see only grass.

'I can't believe he shot you!' Shara gasped, and looked behind her. 'Oh no, he's coming over!'

Jess swung an arm at her. 'He didn't shoot me, you idiot,' she lisped through her swelling mouth. 'Dodger headbutted me. I told you he was dangerous.'

'Jessy, I'm so sorry. I shouldn't have . . .' Shara looked over her shoulder again.

'You shouldn't have just taken off like that,' Jess shrieked. 'What is with you lately?'

Shara tried to help her up. 'I didn't mean to . . .'

'Dodger has been playing up all day, or haven't you noticed?' Jess pulled herself up off the ground and pushed Shara with both hands.

Shara staggered backwards. 'Hey!' she yelled. 'I was trying to cheer you up!'

'By putting me on some half-wild brumby and nearly getting me killed?'

43

'No. I . . .'

'Just get away from me.' Jess's face was throbbing so hard she could barely think straight. Behind Shara, she saw Lawson Blake turn on his heel and walk away. She did the same, heading towards home.

Shara called after her. 'Jess! Wait! You're bleeding!'

'*Leave me alone!*' Jess screamed.

7

WHEN JESS ARRIVED HOME, Caroline had fifty conniptions. She buried Jess's swollen face under a packet of frozen broad beans and raced her off to the closest hospital. After several hours in the waiting room among vomiting, bleeding and groaning people, Jess was sent home with a fresh icepack and some painkillers and told to rest for a week.

Craig hit the roof. First he rang Shara's mum, ranting about Shara being so irresponsible. Then he stormed down to the police station to have Lawson Blake arrested.

The next day the police paid a visit to Lawson, who came up with some half-baked story about his cattle – the same story that he phoned Craig with afterwards, smarmily apologising and inviting him over to 'discuss it'.

Now, two days later, her parents seemed to think Jess was having some sort of breakdown because of Diamond.

Her father was making appointments with school counsellors and psychologists, while Caroline insisted she needed a spiritual healer. Jess was refusing point-blank to go and see any of them. With only a week left until the summer holidays, she told her parents she would be fine so long as she had that week off school.

Buzz rumble.

Shara: we need to talk

Jess flipped her phone shut.

'I hope she gets into that stupid school,' she grumbled to herself. 'I hope I never have to talk to her again! For at least a month!'

Jess would be only too happy to lock herself in her bedroom and never come out again, but her parents were adamant that she keep up with her chores, and for some perverse reason that included looking after Dodger. Some stupid 'getting back on the horse' way of thinking – obviously thought up by someone who had never ridden a horse, let alone fallen off one, and definitely had never been headbutted by a total psycho like Dodger.

But her protests only earned her a karmic forgiveness lecture from Caroline. 'You must cultivate love, darling; fight evil with goodness. Don't destroy yourself with anger.'

The lecture made Jess feel even crankier. In the end she gave up protesting, choosing instead to storm to her room and count her miseries. She couldn't believe they'd listened to that Lawson Blake. They needed to wake up and smell the gunpowder.

In the afternoon, at her father's insistence, she set about fixing the fence that Dodger had broken. Hateful creature!

She pulled some pliers from her back pocket and twisted the wire back to keep it off the ground. That horse just had no respect for fences. He had no respect for anything.

Two horses walked down the road towards her. She recognised their riders: Rosie and Grace Arnold from Valley View Pony Club. The two sisters had the same tawny-blonde hair, olive skin and brown eyes. She had seen them at gymkhanas many times but had never actually spoken to them. In Coachwood Crossing, everyone knew everyone. Or at least, everyone knew everything *about* everyone.

Jess knew that the Arnolds had a stud farm and bred Australian stockhorses. Rosie was the elder sister and she always rode a chestnut horse called Buster. Grace was younger and never rode the same horse twice. Their stud farm, Jess imagined, must be huge.

Rosie sat neatly in the saddle with her heels down

and her back straight. A short riding crop sat at a perfect angle across her thigh and a tidy plait poked out below her helmet. Buster's saddlecloth was clean, blue and matched his shin boots.

Grace wore jeans that looked like they had been worn for days. She held her reins in one hand and kicked her gangly-legged grey horse up into the uneven trot typical of a freshly started mount.

As the sisters approached, it became obvious they were going to stop and say hello. Jess considered fleeing but realised she had left her run too late.

Oh, great, I look like the elephant man.

'Hi.' She looked away, trying to hide her face.

'Hello,' said Rosie, bringing her horse to a halt. Both girls loosened their reins and allowed their horses to stretch their necks and pick at the grass. 'Horse go through the fence?'

Jess fiddled needlessly in her pocket. 'A rather large goat, actually. Probably wanted to pick at the lucerne trees.'

'You're Jess, aren't you? You go to Coachwood Pony Club.'

'Yep.' Jess couldn't justify fiddling in her pocket any longer and looked up. 'Rosie and Grace, right?'

'Kwor! What happened to your eye?' Grace gawked shamelessly.

'Yes, I'm Rosie and this is my sister, Grace. Sorry about her.'

Grace barged on, ignoring Rosie. 'So what happened?'

'A horse reared up in my face.'

'Did you fall off?'

'No.'

Grace looked approving.

'We were really sorry to hear about Diamond,' said Rosie.

'Yeah, that sounded terrible,' said Grace. 'We couldn't believe it when we heard about it.'

'We used to love watching her jump at gymkhanas. She could jump so high for such a small horse,' said Rosie. 'We used to run over and watch when your name was called.'

'And you guys were amazing at mounted games,' Grace chipped in. 'How do you do all that vaulting on and off?'

'Grace is your secret admirer,' said Rosie.

'As if!' Grace snorted and then changed the subject. 'So, are you going to get another horse?'

Jess shrugged. 'Dunno.'

Buzz, rumble.

Jess ignored it.

'You're so nosy, Grace,' said Rosie.

'What?' said Grace. 'It's just a question.'

Rosie looked at Jess. 'You're *so* lucky you don't have to put up with a little sister.'

'Umm.' Jess wasn't sure what to say. 'So, what did you hear about Diamond's accident? Who told you about it?'

'Tegan Broadhead reckons she was stuck in the cattle grid for hours and there was blood everywhere and her legs were nearly ripped right—'

'*Grace!*' Rosie hissed.

Grace quickly changed tack. 'But I wouldn't believe anything Tegan says. She's a real troublemaker.'

Jess steeled herself. She had to know the details. 'Was Tegan there? Did she say how Diamond got out of her paddock in the first place?'

The two sisters went quiet.

'What?' Jess pressed. 'You know something. What happened?'

'No, really,' said Rosie, 'that's all we heard. They said that she was found lying in the cattle grid and she was badly injured. Was that your phone before?'

'It was Shara Wilson's horse that hunted her through the cattle grid. Tell her about that,' said Grace.

'What?' Jess was stunned. '*Rocko?*'

Katrina's words echoed in her ears.

Why don't we just toss it out onto the river flats and let other people's horses chase it through a cattle grid?

Rosie turned to her sister and spoke with gritted teeth.

50

'Grace! Tegan was just making trouble when she said that. Don't go spreading stuff around when it's probably not true.'

'But Tegan said she saw it,' said Grace. 'So did Katrina.'

'They saw it? What? Were they there when it happened?' Jess pressed urgently for more.

Buzz rumble.

She flipped her phone open impatiently.

Shara: meet me down at drover's yards, jess, pleeease!!!

Jess's mind raced back to the accident.

Where was Rocko? I didn't see him. Where was he?

She stared at the screen of her phone. Surely it couldn't be true.

Jess looked up at Rosie. 'Were Tegan and Katrina there when it happened?'

'They were passing on gossip, that's all,' said Rosie. 'I don't know for sure if they were there or not. But I do know that I wouldn't trust anything they had to say. They're trouble, those two – nasty trouble.'

Jess tried to untangle her thoughts. She didn't know what to believe. Five days ago her life had made perfect sense. Now it was all jumbled. She just couldn't believe that Shara would keep something like that from her. She wouldn't just leave Diamond lying in a cattle grid. Jess opened her phone, brought Shara's message back up and punched in a direct question.

did rocko chase diamond thru that grid?

She snapped her phone shut and stared back up at Rosie and Grace. 'I'd better get back to fixing this fence,' she said in a tight voice. 'I'll see you around.'

'You can tighten that wire up with a stick. Want me to show you?' said Rosie, slipping off her horse and picking a stick up off the ground, which she began to twist around the wire. 'This is an old bushie's trick that Harry taught me.'

'Who's Harry?'

Jess watched Rosie turn the stick like a tap. The strand of wire began twisting around and around itself, pulling tighter and tighter.

'He's our uncle,' said Rosie.

'Yeah, that's where we're going now,' said Grace, 'if we ever get there.'

'He breeds stockhorses. We're just on our way to see his foals. He has eight of them.' Rosie stood back and viewed the fence with a satisfied look on her face. 'Hey, why don't you come with us? Come and see the foals.'

'Yeah,' said Grace. 'They are sooo cute.'

'Thanks, but I don't have a horse to ride.'

'You could walk,' shrugged Rosie. 'If you get tired, you can jump on the back of Buster.' She gave her horse a slap on the rump. 'He's real comfy!'

Jess's head was still reeling with images of Rocko chasing Diamond. 'Hey?'

Rosie patted Buster's rump again.

'I look like a freak,' said Jess.

'Don't worry about it. The foals won't care,' said Rosie.

'Maybe next week.'

'Nup,' said Rosie. 'You gotta see them when they're newborn. They won't be the same in a week. They won't be all funny and wobbly.'

'Just jump on Buster,' said Grace. 'He won't hurt you. He's built for comfort, not speed – that's what Dad reckons!' She began making pig noises.

'Shut up, Grace,' grumbled Rosie.

'Well, I'm kinda grounded too.' Jess could hear herself making excuses. That last one wasn't even true. But she hadn't planned on having a good day today. She had planned on being miserable. Right now she was downright angry.

'Okay, but we better get going, because we told Harry we'd be there before lunch,' said Rosie, putting her foot in the stirrup and climbing back on her horse.

'Wait. I just . . .'

She just what? What was her problem? Was she seriously planning to miss out on eight newborn foals?

'Hang on. I'll get my bike.' Jess switched her phone off and shoved it back in her pocket. She could think about Shara later.

8

AFTER AN HOUR'S ride over bumpy and sometimes steep trails, Jess was glad to get off the bike. She propped it up against the fence and squeezed her aching butt cheeks together. What a torture rack!

From behind her, Grace giggled. 'Give me a horse and saddle anytime!'

Jess wiggled her legs, purely for Grace's amusement, and then unlatched the gate for them to bring their horses through.

Inside was a set of timber cattle yards adjoining a full-size rodeo arena. Next to it was a huge barn, and beyond that stretched acres of green pasture. Sitting on the top rail of one of those yards was an old man wearing a battered old hat.

'Hi, Harry,' Grace and Rosie chorused.

Harry answered in a voice as croaky as a cane toad's.

'Hey! How you going, girls? Come and see the colts!'

Rosie and Grace tethered their horses and jumped up onto the timber slab fence. Jess followed. In the yard, two teenage boys sat on jet-black colts. The horses' coats shone like glossy patent leather. Both had large, soft eyes and handsome heads, but one had a small white star on his forehead and a snip on his nose, while the other had no face markings but did have small white socks on his hind feet.

Rosie glanced down at her from the fence and grinned. 'They're twins – pretty special, hey?'

'Who, the boys?' asked Jess.

'No, the horses,' laughed Rosie. 'The boys aren't even brothers.' She pointed to the taller of them. 'That's Tom, on Nosey. He stays here during the holidays. Private-school boy – he gets to break up from school earlier than us. Both his parents are lawyers and they're always working.' She bent down and whispered, 'They are so rich. You should see all the gear he has for riding. His saddle cost four thousand dollars!'

Jess made a choking sound. 'Four thousand bucks? I didn't know you could pay that much for a saddle!'

'Yep, you sure can,' said Rosie. 'Anyway, Tom doesn't care about all that. He lets me ride with his saddle all the time.'

'Cool,' said Jess, wondering what a four-thousand-dollar saddle would feel like to ride in. 'So who's the other one?'

'Oh, that's Luke, on Legsy.' Rosie seemed to have trouble tearing her eyes away from Tom. 'He came here to do a brumby-gentling program a few years ago, and he was so good with horses that Harry asked him to stay. He's a foster kid.' She lowered her voice to a whisper again. 'He was a real mess when he first came here. He used to come home from school all busted up from fighting. Harry doesn't make him go to school anymore – reckons he's better off working with the horses and doing something he's good at.'

Harry interrupted their whispering. 'Are you going to introduce me to your friend, Rosie?'

Jess looked at the ground.

'Jess, this is Harry,' said Rosie.

'G'day, Jess!' said Harry. He pulled a chewed toothpick from his mouth and flicked it onto the ground. 'How do you like my colts?'

'They're like something out of a movie. They're beautiful.'

'They're twins. First I've ever had survive,' said Harry. He looked proudly at the two colts.

'They're the first twin horses I've ever even seen,' said Jess.

'Want to see them draft some cattle?' asked Harry.

'Umm . . .' Jess wasn't really sure what 'draft some cattle' meant. She remembered that Shara had talked non-stop about something called campdrafting when she came back from a holiday in Darwin once. She was so taken with the sport that she had spent the next month chasing her parents' purebred Droughtmaster cattle up and down their hilly property, despite their demands that she stop. Her dad had eventually grounded her.

Harry didn't wait for Jess to answer. 'Cut out a beast, Tom,' he yelled, then turned to Jess and patted the fence rail. 'Hop up, kiddo. You won't see much from down there.'

Tom nodded briefly at Harry, and rode the horse into a yard full of cattle.

Jess climbed up onto the rail. She watched Tom single out a big, ugly cow and push it away from the mob. It trotted to the top of the yard, moaning loudly in protest, and then tried to dart back to the mob. Quick as lightning, the colt swung to the left and blocked its path. The heifer lunged to the right, only to have the colt spin on its heels and block it again.

'Real cowy, these colts,' Harry muttered as he climbed off the rail and opened a big set of gates. The cow lifted its heels and gave a clumsy skip with its hind legs as it bolted out of the arena. Tom held the colt steady as he cantered after it.

'Go easy now, Tom. Just track after it for a bit,' Harry called out.

After following the cow for a minute or so, Tom reined the colt in and brought him back to the others. Tom was as tall and gangly as the colt he rode and his white teeth were the only part of his face Jess could make out under his black helmet.

Luke gave his horse a nudge to make it step forward. He had the crumpled appearance of a teenager who did his own washing. Rusty-brown hair poked out from his helmet and his face was covered in freckles. 'Want me to put Legs around, Harry?' he asked.

'Sure, Luke, let's see what he can do,' said Harry, opening the gate and waving him into the yard.

Luke walked the horse into the yard. He lifted the rein slightly and clicked it up. The colt bounded to the left as if on springs. With barely a shift in the saddle, Luke commanded it to halt, reined it back again and sent it leaping to the right as he singled out a cow.

'Not a bad rider, ay?' Harry winked at Jess. 'That's the more flighty of the two colts. Luke keeps 'em steady.'

Harry swung the gates open and let Luke, the colt and the cow into the large arena. He watched them work with a satisfied look on his face.

Then he turned to Jess. 'Come on, Jess, I'll show

you their sire if you like.' And just assuming she *would* like, he limped towards the arena gate, calling back to Tom and Luke, 'Righto, boys, that's probably enough for now.'

'Are you going to show Jess Biyanga?' asked Grace, jumping from the fence. 'I wanna come too.'

'Me too,' said Rosie.

'Get those horses watered first,' said Harry. He motioned for Jess to follow him towards the barn.

Inside the big timber barn were twelve stables. The walls were built from hardwood slabs, thick enough to withstand a double barrel from a horse's hind legs, and high enough that even a tall horse couldn't see over them.

As Jess caught up, Harry glanced sideways at her. 'So, what happened to your eye?'

At that very moment Katrina Pettilow emerged from a stable, leading Chelpie behind her. Every horse in the building immediately started whinnying and fidgeting.

Jess immediately forgot Harry's question and confronted Katrina. 'You saw Diamond's accident happen, didn't you?'

Katrina stared in disgust at Jess's face. 'No,' she said, and turned away.

'You did, I know you did,' said Jess. 'Why don't you just tell me what happened?'

'Why don't you ask your best friend?' snorted Katrina.

'Best keep that mare away from the stallion, Katrina,' interrupted Harry. 'She in season or something? She's upsetting all the other horses.'

Katrina kept her back to Harry and didn't answer. She tethered Chelpie to a piece of hay twine that hung from the stable door. Jess felt a twinge of satisfaction when she saw that Chelpie's tail still had a hint of green to it.

'This way,' said Harry. 'So, what happened to your eye?' he repeated.

'A horse banged his head in my face.' Jess answered quietly so that Katrina wouldn't hear her. There was something about Harry that she instantly trusted. Katrina Pettilow, however, was a different story. She glanced over her shoulder and saw her brushing Chelpie. Jess wished she'd had more time to grill Katrina before Harry led her away.

'Hmmm,' said Harry.

At the end of the stable aisle was a loosebox. It was twice the size of the others and had a door opening out into a large yard at the back. Harry pointed at the adjoining feedroom. 'Pick me out a nice big biscuit of hay, would you, Jess?' He unlatched the stable door and called out, 'Hey, big daddy-o!' He motioned for Jess to take the hay inside. 'In you go.'

A fat black and white pig came trotting into the stable, grunting and squealing. He nudged at Jess, demanding the hay, and nearly bowled her over. She gave a surprised laugh. 'Is this Biyanga?' she asked, fighting off the hungry pig as it ripped at the hay and made it spill all over the stable floor.

'That's Grunter, his stablemate. Ryan saved him from the dogs on a hunting trip and gave him to Annie – that's the missus – to fatten up for Christmas.' He laughed. 'Nice gesture, but we don't have a sty. I had to lock him in here or Annie was gonna stick him in the freezer.' Harry rolled his eyes. 'Biyanga's fallen in love with him. He won't go anywhere without his pig. He comes to all the campdrafts with us.'

Jess gave the pig a scratch along his back and he wriggled with delight.

Who's Ryan?

At that moment, the stallion walked in.

He was hooded and rugged so that all Jess could see were four jet-black legs poking out from below his rugs, a black nose with white markings, and the same soft, kind eyes as the colts. He gently nuzzled the pig, then pushed it away from the hay. It squealed in protest.

'They're like an old married couple, can't live with or without each other,' said Harry. He hobbled into the stable and began to unbuckle Biyanga's rug. With one big pull from the back end, it slid off into his arms, unveiling the most impressive horse Jess had ever seen.

He was the stuff dreams were made of: as black as black, with a thick, wavy tail, powerful hindquarters and flawless straight legs. He had a long, elegant neck and a perfectly symmetrical, thin white stripe running down his face.

Harry stood back and admired him. 'What do you reckon?'

'He's so fat he can hardly walk,' said Grace, appearing at the stable door. 'Look, he's got cellulite on his bum.' She giggled, ducking a swipe from Harry.

'Cheeky little brat,' he chuckled.

Jess stepped forward and ran a hand over Biyanga's glossy neck. He squealed suddenly and rushed to the door, slamming her against the wall of the stable. She lost her footing and fell into the sawdust, just inches from the stallion's front feet.

Harry took a step forward, placing himself between Jess and the stallion. 'Easy does it, fella,' he soothed. 'She's not for you.' He reached a hand down to Jess and pulled her up, and then turned to Katrina. 'I've told you ten times not to bring that mare in here while she's in season.'

'She's not *in* season,' argued Katrina. 'And I need to talk to you about her stable.'

'Well, you don't need to bring the horse with you. Get her out of here now.'

'Her stable is filthy,' said Katrina, ignoring him. 'She's a true white. We've paid all this money and . . .'

Biyanga let out another short cry and lunged at the door with his teeth bared. Chelpie squealed and rushed towards him, ears back.

'Didn't you hear me?' said Harry. 'I said, *get her out!*'

Then he turned to Jess and looked anxiously into her face. 'You all right, kid?' he asked. When she nodded, he breathed a sigh of relief. 'I thought you were gonna pass out on me for a minute there.'

Jess managed a smile and said, 'I'll be okay.'

Harry guided her to the stable door. 'Hang on a minute.'

In the aisle there was a clatter of hooves on concrete. Katrina pulled on Chelpie's lead rope, but the mare was too strong for her. The rope slid straight through her hands and she fell over backwards, narrowly missing a fresh pile of poo.

Grace came out of nowhere and made a dash for the mare's rope. She pulled Chelpie to one side, flicked the tail of the rope at her flank, making her turn away from the stallion, and led her out of the stables.

'Give me back my horse,' Katrina yelled angrily after Grace. She clambered to her feet and accosted Harry. 'I was coming to speak to you about my horse's welfare. Her stable—'

Harry interrupted her. 'Her stable is cleaned every morning, Katrina. If you had any concern for your horse's welfare, you'd let her out into the paddock for the day so the poor thing could have a pick of grass.'

Katrina's face went tight and pointy. 'I've told you before – she gets too wild when she's out in a paddock. She gets through fences and tries to escape to the river. She needs to be stabled. That's what we're paying you for.'

Harry stared at her with disbelief and lowered his voice to a slow growl. 'Now you listen to me, kid. This is my property and I make the rules – mostly for the safety of my guests. If you can't obey those rules, then I suggest you find somewhere else to keep your pure white pony.' He stood up and walked back towards Biyanga's stable.

Katrina marched back down the aisle. She snatched Chelpie's lead rope from Grace and tugged. 'Come on, Chelpie.'

Grace pulled a face at Katrina's back. 'Poo-magnet!' Then she walked back to Biyanga's stable. 'Are you all right, Jess?'

Jessica opened the stable door, leaning on it to keep her balance as she swung it back and bolted it shut. 'Yeah, I'm okay,' she said flatly. Her whole head throbbed. 'I might go and sit down for a bit.' She felt angry at herself for being such a sook. She didn't want to see the foals anymore. She just wanted to go home.

Every time she went near a horse these days, she was a total disaster. What was she thinking, coming over here with a bunch of people she didn't know?

She pulled out her phone and switched it back on.

Mum, can u pick me up?

Before Jess could switch it off again, the phone rumbled in her hand.

She glared at it for a moment, then pressed the view button.

Shara: yes, but I can explain, pleeease, we have to talk!!

Jess's first instinct was to smash the phone on the concrete floor. Instead, she sank to the ground and sobbed.

9

ON SUNDAY MORNING, Jess rolled over in bed and stared at the clock. It was six o'clock. She'd had a weird dream that three bright lights were chasing her through a paddock, calling her name.

The sound of hooves clattered beneath her window.

Shara?

Since yesterday's text message, Jess had blocked her – from her phone, from email, from Facebook, and any other possible place she could think of.

If she thinks I'm going to talk to her, she's wrong.

She pulled herself up onto her knees and peeked out through the curtains. At the bottom of the verandah steps, Grace sat on a brown horse, looking like a turtle with her neck craned forward and an overstuffed pack on her back. Jess tossed off her doona and shuffled to the front door, squinting in the sunlight.

Grace motioned for her to come outside. 'Your hair

has gone crazy,' she noted as Jess reached the bottom step.

'Well, I'm still half asleep,' Jess grumbled. 'Do you always get up this early?'

'Harry's registering the foals today,' Grace replied.

'I guess that's a yes.'

'He lets Rosie and me help to name them. And we found that mare that went missing down on the river flats. She had her foal and it's an Appaloosa!' she said excitedly.

'What mare that went missing?'

Grace lowered her voice and said in a dramatic tone, 'The foal looks a bit like Diamond!'

Jess immediately woke up. 'Wait for me.' She ran back up the stairs and rummaged through the knee-deep squalor that was her bedroom. 'Joddies, joddies, where are my joddies?'

Hastily dressed, she crept into her parents' room and whispered to her snoring father. 'Dad!'

'What is it, honey?' asked Caroline from the other side of the bed.

'Can I go with Grace Arnold to look at the foals again? There's one that looks like Diamond!'

'At this hour of the morning?' said Caroline.

Craig opened his eyes. 'Where exactly are you going?'

'To Harry's place, to look at the foals. I went there yesterday, remember? There's a new one that looks like Diamond.'

Craig sat up. 'Who's Harry?'

'He's Grace and Rose's uncle.'

'Harry who? What's his last name?'

Caroline saved her. 'They're nice girls, Craig. We know them from pony club. Go on, Jess. But have some breakfast before you go.'

Jess flew out the door before her father could object.

When they arrived at Harry's, Rosie, Tom and Luke were sitting on bales of hay on the back of a ute. Rosie waved enthusiastically. 'Hurry up,' she called. 'We're about to go!'

Jess dumped her bike and ran to the ute. She climbed up next to Rosie, slipped on a loose biscuit of hay and somehow landed in Luke's lap. 'Oh, sorry!'

Luke grinned but said nothing while she tried to climb off him.

Harry hobbled down from the house with a clipboard and pen. He saw Jess clambering off Luke and gave her a wink.

What? I wasn't . . . I was just . . . I was not!

She climbed over Rosie and found a spot on top of a hay bale. It didn't feel overly secure, but it was as far away as possible from the boys.

'That's one way to introduce yourself, I s'pose,' said Harry as he reached for the driver's side door, and before Jess could protest, he said, 'Righto, who wants to come down the paddock and help me register this season's foals? We've got to get a record of all their markings and colour and so on and so forth. Details, details, endless details . . .' His voice trailed off into a mutter as he lowered himself into the front seat.

Grace ran out from the stables. 'Wait for me!'

'You give that horse some water?' Harry asked as he leaned over and opened the passenger door for her. Grace nodded as she jumped in. The ute roared to life, and soon they were bumping their way down a long laneway with fences and horses on either side.

At the end, the mares cantered up to the gate, eager for some hay. The foals followed on awkward, jerky legs, frolicking and bucking. Harry drove around the paddock in a big circle and the mares flocked around as the girls tossed out hay in biscuits. As the horses settled into feeding, Harry pulled on the brake and got out his clipboard.

Luke grabbed some tools from the back and without a word, headed towards a leaky water trough. Tom jumped over the side of the ute and followed.

Harry shuffled through his papers. 'Let's start with Elly's foal,' he said. He hobbled towards a brown mare.

She nickered softly to him as he ran a hand over her shoulder, checking her brands and marking them down in his notes. 'What've you got for us this year, Elly?' He turned to the girls. 'Is that foal gonna be bay or black, Rosie?'

'Black for sure, Harry. Look around its eyes!' said Rosie. Sure enough, its brown foal fluff was beginning to shed, revealing glossy black circles around its eyes.

'Sure it's not buckskin?'

Rosie tossed a piece of hay at him.

'Okay, if you say so. Black it is!' he chuckled, writing it down in his notes. 'Geez, what day was it born? I think this one was born last Saturday, wasn't it?'

'It's a colt, Harry. Let's call him Biggles,' said Grace.

'No, it has to be an Aboriginal name like Biyanga,' said Rosie.

'What does Biyanga mean?' asked Jess.

'It's an Aboriginal word meaning "father",' explained Harry. 'When Biyanga was born he presented backwards, and an Aboriginal stockman helped me to turn him.' He shook his head. 'Bloody amazing horseman, he was. He saved the foal *and* the mare so I asked him if he'd name the foal. He said the colt would grow up to be a great sire, so he called him Biyanga.'

Rosie grinned at Jess. 'Good name, isn't it?'

'I reckon,' said Jess.

'Let's call this one Billabong!' Rosie suggested.

'Billabong: I like that,' said Harry, writing it down. 'We could call him Billy for short.'

They went from mare to mare, recording their brands, colour and markings, and thinking up worthy names for the foals. They called a chestnut colt Boomerang, a black colt Corroboree, and black filly Coolamon.

As they went about naming and recording details, the foals stayed close to their mothers, nuzzling udders for milk or just taking shade in their shadows. From beneath a chestnut mare, Jess could see a small muzzle snuffling for its mother's teat. Its little round chin was covered in long wiry hairs.

She bent down on one knee so that she could get a closer look. As another mare brushed past its rump, the foal scrambled beneath its mother, and popped out in front of Jess with a confused expression. It looked straight into Jess's eyes and paused, cocking its head to one side.

Jess held her gaze. 'Beautiful girl,' she whispered.

Then the filly trotted unsteadily around to face its mother again, displaying a white snowcap marking over the rump of its chestnut body.

Jess felt a rush of joy. For that brief moment, while the little animal stared into her eyes, all the fractured and broken pieces of her soul came back together, making her feel complete. She was connected to something again.

Somehow this filly was a part of her. It was bizarre.

'She's a little Appaloosa,' said Rosie. 'Her colour was a complete surprise to her owners. They thought the mare was just a solid colour, but if you look, she's got a few speckles here and there. Harry reckons she's an Appaloosa too, but she just has minimal markings.'

'Why doesn't Jess name this one?' suggested Harry. 'There's something special about her, don't you think?'

'Won't her owner want to name her?' asked Jess.

'Nah, he just wants her registered.'

Jess thought about it. There was indeed something very special about her. 'How about Walkabout?' she asked.

'She's been walkabout all right,' laughed Harry. 'She gave us a real run-around down on the river flats. We couldn't find her for days.'

'That's a perfect name, Jess,' said Rosie. 'We can call her Wally for short.'

'Walkabout it is,' Harry said, writing it down. Then he scratched his chin and said thoughtfully, 'She's an old soul, that one.'

'What day was she born?' asked Jess.

Harry thought about it and said, 'Last Tuesday, probably . . . no, last Wednesday. That's right. The mare went missing after the Wednesday feed delivery.'

Jessica's heart skipped a beat. That was the day

Diamond had died. She couldn't help feeling that there was some weird link between Diamond and the little filly, something Jess couldn't quite put her finger on, the way she made her feel, the familiarity with which she looked at her. It was haunting.

'You look as though you've seen a ghost,' said Harry.

'It's like she knows me or something,' said Jess.

'She's the pick of the bunch, I reckon,' he said. 'Shame I don't own her.'

Behind Harry, Jess saw Grace crawling on her hands and knees among the herd, gaining the curiosity of one of the more inquisitive foals. She sat cross-legged, letting the foal come up and sniff her head, while she stayed perfectly still.

Rosie shook her head. 'She's gonna get herself killed one day.'

While Grace and Rosie decided on their favourite foals and tried to get close enough for pats, and the boys patched up some holes in the fence, Jess couldn't take her eyes off the chestnut Appaloosa filly.

She walked home that afternoon feeling alive for the first time in days. A million thoughts rolled around in her brain, all leading back to the filly. That funny little look she gave her before she displayed her rump. Jess wanted to go back and see her again. She really wanted to tell Shara about her.

Jess reached for her phone, then realised she hadn't brought it — and anyway, she wasn't talking to Shara. She could just miss out!

10

BIYANGA WANDERED CASUALLY into the stable with Grunter frolicking about his legs. It was the following weekend and Jess had woken early, unable to sleep again, thinking about Walkabout. As soon as the sun peered over the horizon, she'd slipped into a pair of jodhpurs and headed for Harry's place. She emptied some grain into the stallion's feedbin and stuffed his haynet full. From the stables on top of the hill she could see across Harry's whole property.

Shara would love this.

The mares and foals were scattered about their paddock, some grazing and some sleeping. Others groomed their foals and urged them to stay close. Jess could see the snowcap rump of Walkabout poking out from beneath the chestnut mare, while her front end was busy suckling. The filly gave an impatient stamp as she nuzzled and pushed at the udder, bringing down the milk.

Grace appeared at the door. 'Harry said I could have a ride on the colts today!'

'Hi, Grace! Wow, you lucky thing,' Jess said in awe.

'I also brought a couple of new horses that Dad got at the sales. Harry's going to have a look at them. You can have a ride on them, if you want. The bay one looks like a real goer!'

'Yeah, maybe,' said Jess. She wasn't sure about riding any new horses.

'You usually ride with Shara Wilson, don't you? She still your bestie?'

'We just used to ride pairs in the mounted games,' said Jess, fingering the lifeless phone in her pocket. 'We don't talk much anymore.' She changed the subject. 'Where's Rosie?'

'She's still in bed. She is so lazy in the mornings. I always have to feed her horses or they starve waiting for her.'

'Early mornings can be good sometimes,' said Jess. 'It's like having the whole world to yourself for a little while.'

'Me too!' said Grace. 'I love them. Hey, you and I should be besties!'

Jess laughed. 'Sure!'

Harry limped down from the house and opened the door of the ute. 'Who's coming to feed up?' he called out, as the engine roared to life.

Jessica jumped up onto the hay bales in the back. 'Come on, Bestie!' she said to Grace, giving her a hand up.

Soon they were bumping down the laneway, tossing out biscuits of hay to waiting horses.

When they parked in the centre of the mare's paddock, Walkabout trotted into the open with her neck arched and her tail high in the air. She gave a loud, assertive snort, as though she owned the world. Then she bounced into a gallop, rushing over to her friends, pigrooting all the way. As she reached the other foals, she slid to a halt, then spun on one heel and galloped off in another direction, urging them to follow.

'Did you see that?' Harry whistled. 'What a poser!' He leaned against the side of the ute, watching the foals.

Jess laughed as she carried some hay out into the paddock for the mares. Like the sound of a horse munching or the smell of their sweat, watching foals at play was just one of those wonderful, wonderful things in life.

The filly wheeled around to the left and then galloped straight towards Jess. When Walkabout was nearly on top of her, she skidded to a halt and gave a big cheeky snort. She was so close Jess could feel the spray from her nostrils. The filly looked Jess dead in the eye, and for a split second nothing but the two of them existed. Then she let out a whinny, turned and galloped away again.

Dumbstruck, Jess stood there with the hay still in her

arms. The smile on her face stretched to the tips of her ears and she turned to Grace. 'Did you see that, Grace?' she asked excitedly. 'She came right up to me!'

Grace and Harry had both seen it and they laughed out loud.

'Cheeky little blighter,' said Harry.

Jess felt warm all over. It was as though rays of light were glowing through her whole body.

They left the horses to enjoy their breakfast and, as they bounced their way back up the laneway, Jess asked Grace for her mobile number. She pulled her own phone out of her pocket and flipped it open, ready to punch in the new number.

Grace looked a bit awkward. 'Um, I don't have one.'

Jess stalled, surprised. It hadn't occurred to her that some people might not spend their lives attached to a mobile.

'Oh, okay.' She put hers back in her pocket.

Back at the stables, the smell of frying bacon, eggs, tomatoes and mushrooms wafted from the house.

'Smells like Annie's got breakfast ready,' said Harry as he climbed out of the ute and rubbed his belly. He looked at Jess. 'She was a cook out on the stations when I first met her. Fell in love with her cooking as much as the woman herself.' He started walking towards the house. 'Coming?'

'Come on, Bestie,' said Grace. 'It's Sunday-morning tradition to eat breakfast on the verandah!'

'Sounds good to me,' said Jess as she ran after them.

Inside the house, Rosie sat at the kitchen bench supervising the toaster and chatting to an older woman, who Jess assumed was Annie. She had well-groomed hair tied in a bun and skin that was wrinkly and raisin-brown as if it had seen too much sun. She flipped a pan full of eggs over easy as she talked.

Harry, Grace and Jess kicked off their dusty boots and washed up in the laundry before joining them.

'Good morning, sleepyhead,' Grace said to her big sister as she walked into the kitchen. 'About time you got out of bed. I fed your horses for you this morning while you were in Noddy-Noddy Land.'

'I saw that,' said Rosie, switching the toaster off at the wall and retrieving a mangled piece of toast. 'You should have woken me.'

'I tried, and you just kept on snoring.' Grace demonstrated loudly.

At that moment Tom and Luke entered the kitchen.

'Didn't know you snored, Rosie,' said Tom. He wore a fancy-looking shirt freshly smeared with mud. Luke wore a similar shirt, which carried crease marks as though it had just been pulled brand-new out of a packet. Jess couldn't help wondering if Tom had given it to him.

Rosie blushed. She dropped the piece of toast and swiped at Grace, who was still imitating her. 'I do *not* snore, Grace!'

'Ooo, getting all *embarrassed* in front of the *boys*,' teased Grace.

Jess giggled. Rosie always seemed self-conscious around Tom and Luke.

'You snore worse than Grunter,' said Annie as she carried a huge platter through the kitchen. 'Now pick up that toast and put it in the bin before someone walks it through the house. Tom and Luke, for the tenth time, hats off inside the house and put on clean shirts before you come in my kitchen.'

'Sorry, Annie,' said Luke, removing his hat and revealing sweaty hat hair. He gave it a scratch with his other hand. 'Waterpipe broke down the paddock.'

Tom gave him a shove in the direction of the door and the pair of them squeezed back through it together, good-naturedly elbowing and pushing. Jess heard them laughing and wrestling out on the verandah.

Grace screwed up her nose. 'Why do boys always like touching each other so much?'

Jess helped carry the plates of food out to the verandah. There were eggs, bacon and sausages, fresh fruit and some homemade fig and almond bread. Jess planned on attacking the bread first. It smelled heavenly.

She eyed some butter that also looked homemade.

I should bring Annie some of our organic corn next Sunday to make some fritters. And some goat's milk. And some tomatoes. Nah, she probably has heaps of her own tomatoes. Bet she doesn't grow asparagus. I'll bring her some of that . . .

Before long everyone was sitting at the table, fuelling themselves for the day ahead.

As Jess ate, she turned to Rosie. 'You should have seen Walkabout this morning.' The others joined in and soon they were all talking about foals and horses and planning the day ahead.

Once the dishes were done, they headed back down to the stables and began saddling up.

'Could you do me a favour, Jess?' Harry asked, as he limped alongside her. 'I've gotta try to teach that Katrina girl to campdraft.' He sounded noticeably lukewarm about the idea. 'Totally wrong horse for drafting. It spooks the cattle. Something weird about it, can't put my finger on it.' He frowned and shook his head. 'She should keep that horse in the showring where it belongs.'

'How can I help?' asked Jess.

'My son's coming over in a minute to put some new shoes on Biyanga,' Harry continued. 'Could you hold the horse for Lawson while I give Katrina a riding lesson?'

That gun-toting freak was Harry's son?

For the second time that morning, Jess was speechless.

Lawson Blake pulled a beaten felt hat down over his eyes as he stepped out of a shiny new truck. He walked to the back of the tray and acknowledged his father with a nod as he buckled leather chaps around his waist.

Jess stood by, holding Biyanga. She had never seen Lawson close up. He was surprisingly young. She reckoned he must be in his late twenties, which left her wondering just how old Harry was. Lawson was tall and fit-looking, but had the same unfortunate lumpy nose as his father.

Harry nodded to his son. 'How's it going?'

'Busy as a cat burying its business,' Lawson answered, letting it be known he wasn't there for small talk. Without even noticing Jess, he turned to a large toolbox and began rummaging for the right tools. And then, with a pair of pincers and a rasp in one hand, he pointed to a concrete slab beside the stables and commanded, 'Stand him over there.'

Charming as ever.

Jess did as she was told.

Without ceremony, Lawson got to work on the stallion's feet, snipping off the clenches on the outer hoof and pulling the old steel shoes away. He fired up a gas furnace on the back of the truck and tossed a blank shoe into it. When it was glowing red hot he banged it into shape. Jess watched as he pressed the hot shoe to Biyanga's foot, smoke billowing from the hoof's horny outer rim. It left a black mark, indicating where it sat perfectly flush with the hoof.

Lawson nailed the shoes on, giving six perfectly timed taps of the hammer for each nail. *Tap-tap. Tap-tap. Tap-tap.* He flipped the hammer in his hand and used the claws to twist off the protruding points, then stretched the horse's leg forward and, resting it on his knee, bent the clenches over. All this he did in one fluid motion, moving from one step to the next in a series of effortless transitions.

The job was completed in silence. Lawson stopped only briefly with a curt 'Should never pat another man's dog, mate,' when Jess gave his wriggly blue pup a scratch. He grabbed the pup by the scruff of the neck and tossed it back onto the truck.

As Lawson let the fourth neatly shod hoof fall back to the ground, he looked at Grunter, whose head was in a nearby feedbin. 'That pig oughta be slaughtered by now,' he said, as he unbuckled his chaps and threw his tools into a bucket. He strode towards Grunter, who snuffled about, oblivious to the danger coming towards him.

Lawson made a grab for his hind leg and the pig let out an indignant squeal. As quickly and as fluidly as he had shod the horse, Lawson straddled the animal and hogtied it. Jess watched in horror as he brought a knife out from his back pocket and flicked it open.

'No, wait!' she screamed, dropping Biyanga's lead rope. 'I don't think . . . I mean . . . Harry!' she yelled, in a panic.

Lawson laughed. 'What's the matter, never seen a pig's throat cut before?'

'I don't think you're supposed to do that,' Jess stammered. 'He . . . it . . . that's *Grunter*.'

Lawson roared with laughter. He looked down at the struggling pig and gave it a shove on the shoulder with his foot. 'G'day, Grunter!'

From behind her, Harry spoke. 'Crikey, Lawson, leave the poor kid alone!' He glared at his son. 'What the hell is wrong with you?'

Lawson wiped his hands on his jeans and took a step back. 'Yeah, whatever,' he sniffed, closing the knife and placing it back in his pocket. 'Want me to do this pig for you or what? I've got some beef hanging in the cool-room at home. I can hang this one at the same time, if you want.'

'Nah, I'm not gonna eat this one. He's Biyanga's stable-mate now. He's good to have along at the drafts. Keeps the stallion settled.'

Lawson dropped his shoulders and rolled his eyes in disbelief. 'You're joking, aren't ya?' he shook his head. 'It's because Ryan gave it to you, isn't it? Now you think you can't slaughter it.'

'Give it a rest, Lawson. He's your brother.'

'He is not my brother. Just because you wanted to adopt him doesn't mean I ever had to.'

'Let the pig go, Lawson.' Harry turned and walked away.

Lawson watched him walk back to the stables and then turned to Jess. 'Go get the gate for me, kid,' he said in a gruff voice. Only then did he seem to register who she was. He faltered very briefly, then bent down and cut the rope from around the pig's legs. He gave it a swift kick. Grunter scrambled to his feet and scampered away, squealing noisily.

As Lawson drove through the gate, he stuck his head out the window. 'Tell the old man I'll come over during the week and have a look at those foals.' And without so much as a goodbye, he spun his wheels in the gravel and took off out of the driveway.

11

THE NEXT MORNING, Biyanga paced back and forth in his stable, fretting for his pig. Grunter seemed to have gone into hiding after the hogtying incident.

Jess emptied a bucket of feed into his bin. 'Lose your buddy, mate?'

The stallion's body shuddered as he gave another long, sad whinny, and he snuffled his nose into Jess's tummy. Jess scratched his cheeks. 'I know just how you feel, fella,' she said.

'He gets so het up without Grunter around,' said Harry from behind her.

She spun around. 'Do you think he'll come back?'

Harry opened the stable door and came in to console his horse. 'Yeah, I know he's around somewhere, because half of Annie's garden is missing,' he said. 'I just hope that I find him before she does, or he'll end up as a Sunday roast.'

'You wouldn't let that happen, would you, Harry?'

Harry shrugged. 'Not my call, kiddo. It's Annie's pig.' He ran a hand over Biyanga's shoulder. 'And she does love a bite of fresh pork – roasts it in the Kanga Cooker, all dripping with juice and crackling; pretty tasty.' He gave Biyanga a scratch around the ears and chuckled. 'They gotta catch him first, though, don't they, boy?'

'Is Ryan your son?' Jess asked, remembering the conversation between Harry and Lawson, but not sure if a kid was supposed to ask an adult that sort of stuff.

Harry didn't seem to mind. 'Ryan is Annie's boy. He grew up with Lawson. But there's been a rift between them for a while.' A look of disappointment crossed his face. 'And now Lawson's got his nose out of joint because I let Ryan ride Biyanga in a few campdrafts.'

'I wouldn't let someone on my horse either if they were mean like Lawson,' said Jess without thinking. Then she looked up at Harry in alarm. 'Sorry, I shouldn't have said that.'

'Didn't know you had a horse, Jess,' said Harry, ignoring her comment.

Jess picked up the empty feed bucket and turned away from Harry. 'So Ryan's not Lawson's brother at all, they're just stepbrothers?' she asked, trying to steer the conversation back to Lawson. Anything would be better than talking about her own tragic horselessness.

'You got a horse, have you?' Harry repeated.

'My horse . . .' Jess took a deep breath, ' . . . is dead.' She made her way to the stable door and let herself out, thinking that would surely end the conversation.

But Harry followed her out into the stable aisle. 'How'd it die?' he asked, as he coiled Biyanga's halter and rope and hung them on a hook on the wall.

'She got stuck in a cattle grid,' said Jess, tossing her grooming tools into their bag. She saw the realisation wash over his face and instantly knew that he had heard about it. Everyone heard about everything in this town, especially in horsey circles.

'Oh geez, John Duggin told me about that,' said Harry, his voice softening. 'He said it was awful. You poor bloody kid.' Harry grabbed a bucket, turned it over and sat down on it, then reached out for a second bucket, flipped it over and motioned for Jess to join him. He fumbled in his pocket, found a small container of toothpicks and rattled them about, coaxing one out while he waited for her to be seated.

Jess dropped her bag, wandered over and made herself comfortable on the bucket. Maybe he knew what had happened and he was going to tell her about it.

'I had a horse called Bunyip for thirty-two years.' Harry leaned forward on the bucket and began excavating a tooth. 'He was my first horse, and by geez he was a good one. Honest as the day he was born. I used to put all the local kids on him. But I had to go down the Snowies for six months to do some contract mustering and I knew he wouldn't be around when I got back.'

He paused and flicked the toothpick across the aisle. His watery old eyes looked into the distance. 'I didn't want him to suffer, so I got up real early one morning and gave him a good shampooing. I oiled his tail and brushed his mane, then I polished his best show bridle and put it on him.' Harry smiled with pride. 'He always lived like a gentleman and I wanted him to die like a gentleman.'

He paused, ran his tongue over his teeth and reached into his jacket again. 'Took him down the paddock and shot him, I did. Hardest thing I ever had to do in my life. He's buried under that big mulberry tree down the paddock. He used to like eating the berries off it.'

'I buried Diamond next to our coachwood tree. She used to stand under it for hours and rub her neck on it,' said Jess quietly.

The two of them sat in the stable aisle, Harry chewing on a new toothpick, Jess twiddling her hair and looking at the old toothpick that had speared itself into a poo a few metres away. After a while she asked him about something that had been bothering her. 'Do you believe in reincarnation, Harry?'

Harry looked mildly surprised. 'That's a funny

question,' he said. 'Dunno, I never really thought about it.' He drew a neat circle in a patch of dust with his toe as he pondered the question. 'But I always thought the Aboriginal culture of belonging to your country made a lot of sense.'

'How do you mean?' asked Jess.

'Everything in nature is connected. All the animals and birds and lizards and plants, even the wind and the rain. We're all related and we all need each other. It's true of time as well – the past, the present and the future.' He shrugged. 'You just gotta stop and listen and feel; then you know it's true. Sometimes when I'm out bush, mustering, sitting on a horse, I really feel it: the trees and rocks and dust all whispering to me, all soaking into me. Makes me feel alive.'

Jess thought about how she felt when she was alone with the horses in the paddocks: the sounds of the wind and the birds; the movement of the grass and the sun on her skin. What Harry was saying made a lot of sense, but it didn't answer her question.

'So, what happens when something dies?' she asked. 'Do you reckon it gets reincarnated?'

'Some mobs think so, others don't.' Harry crinkled his forehead. 'The fellas I talked to told me that in the creation time, great ancestral spirits walked the earth and rose up to create all the different parts of the natural world, such as rocks and snakes and lizards. They told me that when a woman conceives a baby, a spirit from one of these natural things enters the woman. There are special places, sacred sites, where these spirits come from. And the spirit that enters you, like possum or turtle or whatever, becomes your totem.'

Jess had heard some of the girls at school talking about totems. 'A totem is like a spirit guide, isn't it?'

'No, no,' said Harry. 'It's not like that at all. Your totem gives you duties to carry, obligations to your mob and country. It creates a special kinship with other people of the same totem.'

'So, what happens when you die?'

'The way I understand it, your soul splits into three parts. Your ancestral-soul goes to sky camp, your ego-soul dies and your totem-soul is returned to the spirits of nature.'

Jess let her mind process this information for a while. 'Reckon a really big old coachwood tree could be a totem?' she asked.

'I guess so.'

Jess rubbed her chin. She couldn't help thinking about Diamond and Walkabout and their uncanny connection. It wasn't that they really looked the same. It was just . . . some weird sort of sameness.

Maybe that was it. That was the link. Walkabout was born on the same day that Diamond died . . .

'Do horses have totems, Harry?'

Harry chuckled. 'Everyone seems to believe in something a bit different and something a bit similar.' He smiled at her. 'Even all the mobs have slightly different beliefs.' He put his hand on his heart and leaned towards her. He spoke softly. 'I reckon you should just pay attention to what your own heart is trying to tell you, kiddo. Listen to Mother Nature and hear what she's saying. She'll give you all the answers.'

Jess sat there engrossed in Harry's words. She imagined Walkabout being born, down by the river, down among the coachwood trees. That's where Diamond was buried, right next to a big old coachwood tree. Maybe they had the same spirit or something.

Jess thought of the big old tree in her garden. It was so old and wise, it had to be sacred.

Harry changed the subject abruptly. 'So who gave you that black eye?'

'It was my cousin's horse, Dodger.'

'So, what happened?' asked Harry.

'I tried taking him for a ride and he just kept tossing his head. He wouldn't stop snatching the reins.' Jess decided not to tell Harry that it was his psycho son who caused it. 'Then he went crazy and reared up. He smashed me in the face with his head.'

'Sure gave you a good shiner,' said Harry, spitting his toothpick out and stamping on it.

'It hurt heaps,' said Jess, running her hand over her face. It still felt sore when she touched it.

'How come he tosses his head so much?'

'I don't know. He's just a really stupid horse.'

'No such thing as a stupid horse, mate,' said Harry. 'The difficult ones are usually the smartest.'

'Well, he must be a genius or something, because there was no way I could make him stop it.'

'Why don't you bring him over here one day, and I'll have a look at him for you?'

Jess screwed up her nose. 'I didn't fall off him, so I don't have to get back on him,' she said. 'And anyway, he's not my horse.'

'Fair enough,' shrugged Harry. 'Just thought I'd offer.'

At that moment, Annie sang out for breakfast.

Harry gave Jess a wink. 'Saved by the bell.' He put a hand on her shoulder to haul himself up off the bucket. 'Let's go and eat. I'm starving.'

'I brought some fresh asparagus from our garden,' said Jess, glad to have the subject changed.

'Those mushy green spear things?' asked Harry, pulling a face.

'It's not tinned stuff. I picked it fresh this morning. Mum reckons you'll live forever if you eat asparagus – it's so full of vitamin C! It even cures cancer!'

Oh my God – was that a health lecture that just came out of my mouth? My mother has brainwashed me!

Harry smiled. 'You're a good kid, Jess. You'll always be welcome around here.'

12

THROUGHOUT THE HOLIDAYS, Jess woke each morning with Diamond, Wally and the ancestral spirits on her mind. She couldn't help it; the idea of them being spiritually linked somehow made Diamond's death easier to accept.

When the sun rose she would slip on her old runners, toss some hay to Dodger and jog to Harry's place. She loved helping out around the stables and eating Annie's camp breakfasts. Annie was thrilled with the fresh asparagus. She steamed it gently, and served it on a plate of its own, deeming it too delicious to be chopped and stirred into an omelette. 'Here, have some. It's good for you,' she said to Harry as she piled it onto his plate.

The day's activities were always planned around the breakfast table. At one end Rosie, Grace and Jess would talk about their favourite horses and riding plans for the rest of the holidays. At the other end Harry would sneak his asparagus onto Luke's plate when he thought Jess wasn't looking. He discussed breeding programs, worming schedules and the price of hay with Luke and Tom.

Jess was happiest when she was down at the mares' paddock playing with Wally. Sometimes, while the others were out trail-riding or schooling young horses, Jess would sit under the trees just watching Walkabout. When the little filly fell asleep, spread out in the sun, Jess would lie back and look at the sky through the canopy of the trees, thinking about spirits and listening to the earth.

At other times, Wally would badger her mother to play. And occasionally there were magical moments when curiosity got the better of her, and she would cautiously approach Jess with her nose outstretched and ears twitching. If Jess made eye contact with her, she would skitter away. But if Jess kept her eyes on the ground, the filly would come closer, sniffing the top of her head and nibbling at her ears.

Over the days and weeks, the two of them developed a friendship. Jess watched how the foals played with each other and tried to imitate them. She would walk past the filly, inviting her to follow. Initially Walkabout kept her distance, but gradually she came closer. Jess would change direction every now and then to make sure she had her attention.

This became a game, and eventually Jess could run around the paddock, ducking left and right with Wally trotting merrily behind her. As she grew bolder, the filly would initiate play, giving Jess a playful nip and looking at her with mischief in her eyes. She would shake her head up and down as though laughing, and gallop away.

Hours melted into days, and time in the mares' paddock took on a dreamlike quality. There was never any sense of an afternoon passing but for the gnawing in Jess's stomach when it was time to eat.

A few days before Christmas, Jess heard the ute bumping its way down the laneway. It was late in the afternoon, well after the usual feed time. She could see Lawson in the driver's seat, but the passenger she did not know. She made herself busy, scrubbing at a water trough.

'This lot are the best Biyanga has ever put on the ground,' she heard Lawson say as he got out of the ute. The passenger side door opened and another man got out. They walked out into the paddock to inspect the foals.

'I wasn't expecting that mare to throw a coloured foal,' the stranger said, as they approached Walkabout.

Wally's owner?

The two men began to circle Walkabout and her mother, pushing them towards the corner of the paddock. As Walkabout skittered past, the man tossed a lasso around her neck. She reared against the rope, shook her head and fell heavily on her side. Lawson pounced on her and held her down, while the other man tightened the rope around her throat until her panicky squeals faded. The mare whinnied and paced nervously.

Jess wanted to run and scream at them, 'She can't breathe, you idiots.' She stood helplessly at the trough, watching the filly's eyes roll wildly in terror. Lawson knelt on Walkabout's neck and the stranger ran his hands over her legs, laughing as she kicked out in protest.

'She's a feisty one, I'll give her that,' she heard Lawson say. He pulled something from his pocket and passed it to the other man.

Jess felt sick. What were they doing to her? She moved her head about, but all she could see was Walkabout's legs kicking.

'A bit of the right schooling will soon knock that out of her,' the stranger replied. Then he removed the rope and let the filly struggle to her feet and race back to her frantic mother. The men stood there, hands on hips, talking and watching Walkabout as she whinnied and nuzzled at the mare.

Jess thought they would never leave. She could see a strip of raw skin swelling painfully around Wally's neck where the rope had burned through her fur. There was skin off her shoulder too, where she had crashed so heavily to the ground. Jess longed to touch her, to soothe her and run some cool water over her burn, to let her know not all people were like that.

When the men finally got back in the ute and left the paddock, she quietly approached Walkabout. But the filly and her mother, still shell-shocked, put their ears back and walked away.

It wasn't until later that day, when Jess caught a ride home with Harry, that she heard the terrible news. Lawson wanted to buy Walkabout.

'He *what?*' Jess blurted out, unable to hide her horror.

'Not much I can do about it, Jess,' Harry said as he shifted gear. 'She's not my filly.'

'Who is the owner, then?'

'That was the owner you saw today. He sent the mare up here for stud. Now he doesn't want the foal because it's coloured.'

'What's wrong with her colour?'

'He reckons she doesn't look like a real stockhorse, being Appaloosa,' said Harry dismissively. 'Probably more to do with the mare's papers, though,' he mumbled. 'If she was bred the way he reckons, she would never have thrown a coloured foal. Something amiss there.' He put on the blinker and turned right down Jessica's street. 'That's none of my business, though.'

'What does Lawson want to do with her?'

'He wants to train her for campdrafting. She has enormous athletic ability.'

Jess seethed. It was all wrong. Walkabout was such a free-spirited filly – she would clash awfully with someone like Lawson.

'Why doesn't he buy Billabong? He's going to be a much bigger horse and he'd be much better suited.'

'It doesn't matter about the size,' said Harry. 'Some small horses are much quicker on their feet. The big ones can be a bit clumsy.' He looked across at her. 'You could probably buy her yourself if you could come up with the money.'

'How much is he selling her for?' asked Jess, running a quick calculation through her mind. She had two hundred and forty-six dollars in her savings account and she might get some money for Christmas.

'Two grand. She's got some impressive bloodlines – that's if they're for real.' He pulled over outside Jess's house.

'*What?* Two thousand dollars?' Jess's heart sank. There was no way she could come up with that much money. 'Why does it have to be Walkabout, Harry? There are seven other foals Lawson could choose from.'

Harry gave her a cuff on the head. 'He can't buy her until she's six months old and can be weaned from her mother. So you'll still have a few months before she goes.'

'Thanks for the lift, Harry,' she said glumly, stepping out and grabbing her bike off the back of his ute.

As Jess crawled into bed that night, she felt all the fresh new light that Walkabout had brought into her heart begin to fade. She stared out the open window at the stars that twinkled above the coachwood trees.

What can I do, Diamond?

I'm going to lose Walkabout too.

13

THE NEXT DAY was Christmas Eve. In the morning, Jess helped her mother in the herb patch, picking and bunching thyme for the markets. As she walked between the raised mounds of soil, her feet crushed the mint that crept uninvited onto the pathway, releasing a waft of toothpasty scent. But Jess's mind was on other matters. She had to present a good case to her mother.

She tossed an empty cardboard box onto the pathway, then began.

'Mum,' she said, rummaging through the thyme plants looking for some fresh shoots. If she acted helpful and busy, her mother might be more receptive. 'You know the little foal I told you about?'

'Hmmm.'

'Lawson Blake wants to buy her.'

'So what's wrong with that?' her mum asked, holding a bunch of sprigs and snipping the base into neatness.

'I know you don't like him, but isn't he a farrier? Surely that would be a good home.'

'No, it would be an absolutely terrible home,' said Jess. 'He is *way* too heavy-handed to own a filly like Walkabout.'

Caroline tossed the herbs into the waiting box. 'I'm sure Harry wouldn't let her go to a cruel home.'

'But Lawson has already roughed her up. I saw him. He and another horrible man threw a rope around her neck and nearly strangled her. She was terrified; you should have heard her squealing. She has all these rope burns around her neck and now I can't get near her and—'

'Hey, hey, hang on,' said Caroline. 'Calm down and explain things to me. Why did he rope her? What did Harry have to say about him doing that?'

'Harry doesn't own her, Mum. That other guy does – the guy that roped her. And besides, Lawson is Harry's son, so he wouldn't say anything against him.'

'What!' said Caroline. 'You didn't tell me Harry was related to Lawson Blake.'

'He's nothing like Lawson, Mum.' Jess decided it was as good a time as any to pop the question. 'Can't *we* buy her?'

'Since when has Lawson Blake been Harry's son?'

'I don't know,' said Jess, impatiently. 'Probably since he was born.'

'Yes, well, that makes perfect sense, doesn't it,' said Caroline, rubbing her chin.

Jess resisted the temptation to roll her eyes.

'Mum, this is really important to me. Walkabout is a special horse. She's one in a million. We can't let Lawson Blake get his hands on her. You saw what happened to my face that day. Just imagine what would happen to a horse under his care. We can't let that happen, Mum, we can't.'

Caroline started to pick more thyme. She motioned with her secateurs for Jess to do the same. 'Well, your father and I *were* planning to buy you a new horse after Christmas. But are you sure you want to buy a foal? Wouldn't it be better to buy a horse that you can ride straight away?'

'No, I just want her. It's hard to explain. There's something about Walkabout that is so much like Diamond. Walkabout was born the day Diamond died. She was born under the coachwood trees down on the river. Mum, I think they're . . . spiritually connected.'

Jess looked pleadingly at her mother. Surely Caroline would understand how important this was. 'Diamond was buried under a coachwood tree. That must be their totem, Mum.'

Her mother looked a little confused, but she smiled. 'Are you saying that Diamond has been reincarnated as Walkabout?'

'Well, I . . .' *I sound as kooky as she does.* 'No . . . Well, sort of.'

Caroline smiled. 'I think the karmic yoga has done you good, darling. How much do her owners want for her?'

Here we go . . .

'Two thousand dollars.'

'*Two thousand?* You've got to be kidding!' said Caroline. 'Crikey, Jess, we don't have that sort of money.'

'Not even if we use my savings? I have two hundred and forty-six dollars.'

'We'll get you a new horse, but we really don't have that much money. How about we go looking after Christmas and get you another one?'

'I don't want another one,' Jess said flatly.

'I hate to disappoint you, darling, but *two thousand dollars*? We could put a new engine in the tractor for that. We could do many things with two thousand dollars, and buying a horse isn't high on the list.' Caroline looked at her daughter. 'Besides, you never know what else might come up.'

'What about my education fund that Grand-dad left for me?' Jess asked. It was a last-ditch effort, but she was desperate.

Caroline just gave her a cold *don't-even-think-about-it* stare.

Jess sighed. She picked up the full box of thyme, put it on the back of the truck with the others and pulled out another empty one. There was no point even talking about it. She'd never be able to buy Walkabout.

When Jess arrived at Harry's place later that day, Grace and Rosie were riding Legs and Nosey around the arena. Tom and Luke sat on the rails, yelling instructions to them. Jess walked over and rested her elbows on the middle rail, peering through the slabs of timber.

'Just sit quiet, Rosie,' Tom called out. 'He's still fresh. He might pigroot.'

Rosie answered something Jess couldn't hear and continued walking Nosey around on a light contact.

There was the clink of a metal gate latch and Katrina led Chelpie into the arena.

'Hi, Katrina,' said Jess.

Katrina relatched the gate without answering or turning around.

'Well, that was a waste of breath,' Jess muttered.

Katrina mounted and began circling Chelpie at the other end of the arena. The little mare dazzled with whiteness, even though it wasn't a particularly sunny day. She stretched her perfectly rounded neck down into the bit and walked with such floaty poise that she looked almost surreal.

At the other end, Grace cantered a couple of circles on Legsy and then, with barely a pull on the colt's mouth, she commanded him to slide on his hocks into a halt. Then she lifted the reins to the left and the colt bounced into an easy canter again, loping steadily towards the fence. At the rail, Grace released the reins and gave him a pat, signalling that work was over. Legsy stretched his neck, puffing gently.

Grace looked over at Luke, who was sitting on the rail. 'Can Jess have a ride on Legsy?'

Luke shrugged. 'Wanna ride?' he asked Jess.

She shook her head.

'He's really sensible,' said Grace. 'Come on, if we're going to be besties, you'll have to get back in the saddle soon. You won't have much fun just mucking out stables all the time.'

Jess leaned against the rail. 'Not today, Gracie. I don't feel like it.'

Tom twisted around and looked down at her. 'Why so glum, chum?'

'Harry reckons Lawson is going to buy Walkabout.'

Tom raised his eyebrows with surprise.

'That's bad!' said Grace.

'Lawson can be rough with horses,' said Tom. 'That's why Harry won't let him ride Biyanga.'

'I know,' said Jess, glad that they understood.

'Why would he want Wally?' said Luke, pushing Legsy's head from his lap. 'She'll be too small for him.' He brushed a large blob of white slobber off his jeans and frowned at Grace, who was grinning. 'Get him off me!'

Grace reined the horse back a step.

'Harry reckons it doesn't matter how small she is,' said Jess. 'Sometimes the smaller ones are better on their feet. He says she's the best foal Biyanga has ever produced.'

'Maybe if Lawson can't ride Biyanga, he thinks Wally would be the next best thing,' said Luke.

'He's just trying to get back at Harry for not letting him ride Biyanga,' said Grace.

Tom shifted up the rail towards them. 'Why don't you buy her, Jess?'

'I already thought of that,' said Jess. 'I asked Mum this morning and she said no. Wally's worth two thousand dollars and we just don't have that much money.'

Tom whistled. 'That's a lot of money for a freshly weaned filly.'

Grace called out to her sister. 'Hey, Rosie, did you hear that? Lawson is going to buy Walkabout.'

Rosie rode towards them, a horrified look on her face.

'He was in the mares' paddock yesterday. I saw him

rope Walkabout and nearly strangle her. It was so awful,' said Jess.

'Lawson actually used to be quite nice before he had that big fight with Ryan,' said Grace.

Rosie glanced over her shoulder. 'Something happened in their family, but we're not allowed to know what. Harry gets a bit narky if you ask him about it.'

'Yeah,' said Grace. 'We're too young and stupid to understand, apparently.'

'Well, he probably knows that you'd go flapping your mouth off to everyone if you knew,' said Rosie.

'Would your mum let you have Walkabout if you could find the money?' asked Tom.

Jess shrugged. 'Yeah, I guess so.'

'Well then, somehow we have to find two thousand dollars,' he said.

Jess stared at him. Easy for him to say. His family was rich. If he was in this position, he would just . . .

'Hey,' she said. 'Why don't *you* buy her, Tom?'

Tom grinned and gave Nosey a pat. 'I kinda had something else in mind.'

Jess's face dropped. 'Oh.'

'And besides, you should own her, not me. She's your little buddy.'

Rosie spoke up. 'I think we should unsaddle these horses and have a crisis talk in the tackroom.'

'Yeah,' said Grace, kicking off her stirrups and jumping off Legsy. 'This is really *bad*.'

'The feedroom would be better,' said Luke, climbing down from the rails. 'There's not much to sit on in the tackroom.'

'Yeah, and it's more out of the way, too,' said Tom, turning to glance at Katrina. 'Not so close to you-know-who's stable.'

'Okay, let's put these horses away and meet in the feedroom in ten minutes,' said Rosie, leading Nosey towards the gate.

14

WHEN THE HORSES were hosed off and munching at their haynets, Jessica and her friends gathered in the feedroom. Grace peered down the stable aisle. 'Just checking that the poo-magnet isn't around,' she said, closing the door. 'I think she's gone for a trail ride with Tegan Broadbum.' She sat down next to Jess on a hay bale, wriggling her bottom into place.

Rosie turned a tall white bucket over and inspected its underside. 'That's very unkind, Grace,' she said, dusting off some dirt. She placed the bucket upside down and sat on it.

'I know. It was meant to be.' Grace gave a wicked little chortle and nudged Jess in the ribs.

Jess gave her a semi-distracted grunt of approval. She was too busy imagining Walkabout with whip marks up her flanks, a cut and bleeding mouth and spur welts all over her ribs, as would surely be the case if Lawson Blake bought her.

'Okay, guys,' said Tom, bringing them to order. 'We're having this meeting so that we can help Jess save Walkabout.' He pointed a straw at Jess, getting straight down to business. 'So, Jess, when did you find out about this? Who told you Lawson was going to buy Walkabout?'

She was careful to tell the truth, the whole truth, and not to exaggerate as she told them about Lawson's visit to the mares' paddock with the stranger, and how the two men had roped Wally and forced her to the ground.

'I can't believe anyone could do that to a foal,' said Grace, disgusted. 'There was no need to go anywhere near her.'

'Yeah, that's what bugs me so much,' said Jess. 'It was just so pointless. Now she has terrible rope burns up her neck and she won't let me near her to check if she's okay.'

'Poor little thing,' said Rosie. 'I hope she doesn't think all humans are like that.'

'I hate Lawson,' said Grace.

'You shouldn't say that about your own cousin,' said Rosie.

'Well, he shouldn't be so cruel. I don't care if he's the Queen of Sheba, I hate him,' snorted Grace.

'You mean the King of Sheba,' Rosie corrected her.

Tom interrupted. 'Jess, did you tell Harry about this incident? He's responsible for that mare's care while she's here, and that includes her foal.'

'I did,' said Jess, 'and that's when he told me that the strange man was her owner and that Lawson was going to buy her.'

'Harry does have the right to kick him off the property if he's mistreating the horses.'

'Harry had a look at her neck and said it should heal okay by itself,' said Jess. 'And anyway, I'd rather he didn't do that. The guy would take Wally with him.'

'Good point,' said Tom, looking thoughtful. 'And her price is two thousand, you say?'

'That's what Harry said.'

'Reckon the owner would lower his price?'

Luke spoke up. 'If there are two people bidding for her, he wouldn't lower the price.'

'But she would go to a much better home,' said Rosie. 'Surely that's worth more than money.'

'I don't think the owner cares about that,' said Jess.

Luke spoke again. 'You could make things worse if you bid against Lawson. The price might go even higher.'

Jess was shocked. More than two thousand?

'Do you have any money saved?' asked Rosie.

'Two hundred and forty-six dollars,' Jess replied. 'That leaves one thousand, seven hundred and fifty-four.'

'Oh, is that all,' said Grace.

The feedroom went quiet.

They were wasting their time. Wally was doomed.

'Can you ride?' asked Tom.

'Of course she can ride,' Grace snorted. She turned around and whispered to Luke. 'She's a really good rider. I've seen her at gymkhanas.'

Luke mouthed back, 'Well, how come she never gets on a horse?'

Jess glared at Luke and Grace, who quickly stopped.

'If you knew how to campdraft, you could win some money,' said Tom, pointing his piece of straw at Jess again, as though sizing her up for the task. 'Luke won eight hundred dollars last season. Didn't you, Luke?'

'Yeah, although I would have loved to win out at Longwood – there was fifteen hundred dollars up for grabs in the junior event,' said Luke. 'You gotta be pretty sharp to win out there, though. The kids out that way are born on horses, spend every day mustering cattle.'

Fifteen hundred dollars!

'When is it on?' asked Jess.

'In March. Harry will be taking Biyanga and the two colts,' said Tom. 'I've been training Nosey for months.'

'I'm taking Legs,' said Luke. 'It's a huge draft, twelve hundred head of cattle. We pack up the truck and go for five days.'

'Dad's taking us too,' said Rosie, sounding excited. 'It's one of the biggest drafts in the district. I've never been before. I can't *wait*.'

Grace leapt off her hay bale and faced Jess. 'That's it! Why don't you come too, Jess?' She did a crazy little pogo dance on the spot. 'You could win fifteen hundred dollars!'

'But I don't have a horse,' said Jess. 'And I wouldn't have a clue how to campdraft.'

'Luke'll teach you,' said Tom. He looked at Luke, who shrugged. 'And maybe Harry can find you a horse.'

'I bet I could find you one in our paddocks at home,' said Grace. Then she thought better of it. 'They're all a bit young, though.'

'What about the bay gelding in the yard at your place?' asked Rosie. 'He looks like a stockhorse.'

'No way. That's my cousin's horse. He's crazy.'

'Hey, didn't you say he comes from out west?' asked Tom.

'Yeah, he does,' said Jess. 'He comes from . . .' she paused. 'That's weird. He comes from Longwood.'

Grace gasped. 'Oh my God! It's a sign!' She hopped from one foot to another.

'Jess, I think it might be your destiny!' cried Rosie.

'Hey now, slow down,' said Jess. 'That horse is a rogue. I've only ridden him once and he reared up in my face.' She looked at her friends. 'You all saw my face when

I first came here, right? Well, that was his handiwork.'

'Is *that* how you got the black eye?' asked Tom. 'That was a mean one.'

'Yes, he just kept tossing his head and snatching the reins,' answered Jess, and before she knew it, she was telling them about the day down on the river flats – about Lawson and his gun, Shara being reckless and stupid, the gunshot and Dodger going crazy. Her friends listened with mouths agape. 'I'm telling you,' she concluded, 'he's a total fruitcake.'

'Who are you talking about – Lawson or the horse?' asked Tom.

'The horse,' said Jess.

'Jess,' said Tom. 'Most horses would get a fright if someone let off a gun near them. I reckon it's Lawson who is the fruitcake, not the poor horse.'

Poor horse? Does it matter to no one that Dodger nearly turned me into a pizza?

'Did you give that horse its head?' asked Tom.

Jess gave an exasperated sigh. 'He was tossing his head around way before the gunshot. I have no idea why he kept doing it. He's just stupid, I tell you.'

Four voices chorused back at her in perfect unison. 'There's no such thing as a stupid horse, mate.' If they'd practised for months they couldn't have parroted Harry's voice any better.

'I thought we were here to find a way to help Wally,' Jess said stiffly. 'I don't see what Dodger has to do with that.'

Luke said, 'Why don't you bring Dodger over and try him at campdrafting? Let Harry have a look at him.'

'Okay, okay,' said Jess. 'I'll bring him down here and you can see for yourselves.'

'Attagirl,' said Rosie, leaning over and rubbing Jess's leg.

Jess managed a smile, even though she felt green at the thought of getting back on Dodger.

'Come on!' said Grace, reaching for the door. 'Let's go and ask Harry.'

While the others went to put their horses away, Jess and Grace found Harry in the tackroom, fiddling with an old bridle.

'Hey, Harry,' said Grace, pushing Jess forward into the doorway. 'Jess wants to ask you something.'

'Hmmm,' said Harry without looking up from a tricky buckle that wouldn't come undone.

'I was wondering if you'd have a look at that horse for me.'

'What horse is that, Jess?'

'The one I told you about, the one that reared in my face.'

'Your cousin's horse?'

'Yeah.'

Harry turned and gave her a questioning look. 'What for?'

'To see if maybe I could ride him.'

Harry grinned. 'Good on you, Jessy.'

15

THAT NIGHT, Jess tried her best to muster up some Christmas spirit by helping her parents decorate the tree. Everything had been left late this year. Aunt Margaret had phoned to say her family wouldn't be visiting and without anyone coming to share it, Christmas had nearly been overlooked.

'Talk about doing everything at the last minute,' said Caroline, as she rummaged through boxes of Christmas decorations. 'Fancy not having our tree up. You usually badger us nonstop if we don't have it up on the first of December.'

Jess tried her best to smile. 'I've just had a lot on my mind, I suppose.'

Craig gave her a squeeze. 'You have had a tough year, honey, losing your horse.'

'And my best friend,' said Jess. She didn't know which was worse.

'You haven't lost Shara,' said her mum. 'All you have to do is give her a ring. Why don't you just send her one of those thumb messages with your phone, like you always used to?'

'She lied to me,' said Jess flatly. 'She hid the truth from me.'

'You don't know that, Jess. You haven't even listened to Shara's side of the story. She's your best friend; you should at least hear her out.'

'She didn't even care when my horse got hurt. Now Diamond's dead and I can't ever get her back.'

'Would you do anything to have Diamond back?'

'Of course I would.'

'Would you do anything to have Shara back?'

Jess was quiet even though she knew the answer. She changed the subject. 'I wish Hetty had come. You'd think she'd want to see Dodger. Christmas is going to be a total non-event.'

Caroline sighed and let herself be fobbed off. 'No, it won't; it'll be extra special with just the three of us.'

Later, as Jess tossed about in bed, she thought more about Dodger than the joys of Christmas. She wondered what had made him behave so badly that day on the river flats.

Then she thought of Shara – she knew Rocko had done it, the whole town knew.

She would give her one chance to explain.

Jess rolled over and flicked on the light, then rummaged around in a pile of dirty clothes for her phone. It hadn't been charged for days and was dead as a doornail. She plugged it into the charger and was horrified to remember she had erased Shara's number from her phone book. She didn't know it off by heart.

She fired up her computer, found it in the address book and punched it into her phone.

do u still want 2 talk? I was 2 upset before.
I want 2 no wot hapnd.

Jess collapsed backwards onto her bed and stared anxiously at the phone. Shara always slept with her phone in her hand. She'd answer immediately.

Buzz rumble.

Jess's heart hammered as she flipped her phone open.

systems admin: Your message was unable to
be sent.

'The cow has *blocked* me!'

Jess leapt out of bed and brought up her email. She

had erased Shara's email address too, but *rockorocks@freemail.com* was an easy one to remember. She typed it in, repeated her message and hit Send. But before she could log out, a new message pinged at her. Its subject line read *Returned mail – email address not found.*

On Christmas morning, Jess shuffled out of her bedroom wearily. She'd had an awful night's sleep.

Craig sat in his favourite armchair, fully dressed, drinking coffee. 'Oh, finally!' he said, when Jess walked into the lounge room in her pyjamas, yawning. 'We've been waiting for hours. Come on, I want a prezzie.'

'Can't I get a drink first?' said Jess, rubbing her eyes.

'Here's some fresh wheatgrass juice, darling.' Caroline came out of the kitchen with a glass of green frothy stuff.

Jess grimaced. 'It's Christmas morning, Mum.'

'No? I thought you liked it.'

Jess gave her a pained look.

'What would you like, then?'

'Coke.'

'Stop tormenting your mother, Jess,' said Craig.

Jess chuckled as she reached under the tree and grabbed two presents wrapped in homemade paper with horses drawn all over them. 'Created by my own fair hand,' she said with pride, as she passed one to her father and the other to her mum.

Craig tore at the wrapping and pulled out a pair of huge socks that Jess had knitted in craft classes at school. 'Surfboard covers!' he exclaimed, holding them up.

She laughed. 'You're not supposed to wear them under your shoes. They're more like slippers.'

Her mum picked piously at the wrapping, admiring the drawings before unveiling two pairs of tie-dyed undies that Jess had also made in craft class. 'A beautiful hat!' exclaimed Caroline, pulling one pair onto her head.

'You guys are so childish,' said Jess.

Next, her father leaned over and passed Jess a large flat parcel. 'This is from both of us.'

Jess felt it all over. 'A soccer ball, right?'

'Very funny,' said Craig.

Jess began unwrapping and saw a familiar pair of horse's ears. She stopped with her hand inside the paper.

Caroline shrugged. 'You begged me for it, remember.'

I didn't know how much things would change.

Jess pulled back the wrapper and revealed a large professional photo of herself and Shara at the state championship, on their horses, grinning madly as they held their second-place trophy in the air.

It had been the best and happiest moment of her life. Jess had begged her parents to get her a huge framed

124

copy of it for Christmas. She knew it would have cost them a fortune. She looked at Shara's goofy face and could almost hear the shrieking and laughing the pair of them had gone on with.

How could you betray me like this? We were besties.

Jess wiped at the tears that were sliding uncontrollably down her face.

Caroline shifted around next to her and put a hand on her shoulder.

'I miss her so much,' Jess whispered.

'Shara or Diamond?' asked Caroline.

'Both.' Jess let a few more tears escape and then pulled herself together. She wasn't going to let the past spoil this day for her. It was history. She wiped at her face. 'Sorry, I didn't mean to spoil it for you. Thanks, guys.'

'It's okay, we knew you'd find it difficult to open.' Her mum reached under the tree again. 'Have some more prezzies.' She passed over two bulky parcels wrapped in red paper. Inside one was a new pair of riding boots, and the other contained an Akubra hat.

'Cool! It's just like Gracie's,' said Jess, pulling it onto her head. It was a perfect fit too.

'Not as stylish as mine,' winked Caroline, who still had the tie-dyed undies on her head.

'And there's an envelope for you from Margaret and Paul,' said her dad, passing it to her.

Please let it be money!

Jess pulled out the card and held it in front of her, ready for wads of cash to rain into her lap.

A folded piece of paper fell out, which she read aloud.

Dear Jess,

We were so very sorry to hear about you losing Diamond. As Hetty will be going to university next year, we would like to give you Dodger. We know that no horse is ever as special as your first, but he has always been a reliable mount, and we hope you get the years of pleasure with him that we did. We know you will take good care of him.

Enclosed is a small packet of mulga seeds. They are a fodder tree that we grow out here to feed the livestock. Dodger loves them. We thought they might be nice to plant over Diamond.

All our love,

Auntie Margaret, Uncle Paul, Hetty and Simone

Jess was stunned. They obviously hadn't heard what a disastrous partnership she and Dodger had formed so far. What was worse, there was now no way she could justify buying Walkabout.

Silence fell over the lounge room and they all looked at each other. 'Dodger' had become a dirty word since that day on the river flats.

'You don't have to accept him if you don't want him, Jess,' said Craig.

Jess thought about it for a while. 'It's okay, I've asked Harry to have a look at him anyway.'

Her parents both stared at her in surprise. 'Really? Do you think he's safe?' asked Craig. 'He went mad last time you rode him. Look what he did to your face.'

'I don't know why he behaved so badly for me, Dad,' said Jess. She had been wondering about that all night. 'Harry said he might be able to work out what's wrong with him.'

'I'm not keen for you to ride him all the way to Harry's place, Jess,' said Craig.

'I'll just lead him over. I won't get on him unless Harry thinks it's safe.' Plunging on, she added, 'I need a horse to ride so I can go to the Longwood campdraft in March.'

'The what?'

'The Longwood campdraft. It's a sport where you round up cattle. There's really good prize money.'

'Rounding up cows in Longwood? What on earth are you talking about?' said Craig.

'We thought that I might be able to win enough money to buy Walkabout.'

'Win two thousand dollars? Jess, I don't think you realise how much money that is. Besides, how are you going to get to Longwood?'

'Grace said I could go with her family – they have room for an extra horse on their truck.'

'Jess . . .'

'Dad, I have to give it a shot. It's the only way I can get the money to buy her.'

'But Longwood is a seven-hour drive from here. It's in the middle of nowhere. You can't just pack up and head off in a truck with a bunch of people we barely even know, on a horse that you barely know. What about school? What about your chores? Are you mad?'

Aaargh! Why do parents have to find so many problems with everything?

'Aunt Margaret and Uncle Paul live out there. We haven't been to see them for ages. I thought maybe we could go for a holiday?'

Caroline and Craig exchanged glances. Jess knew her mother had wanted to visit her sister for some time, especially now that they hadn't spent Christmas together. Jess looked pleadingly at Craig, knowing that he was the one she had to win over.

'We could make a holiday of it, Dad. And Dodger could see his old home.'

'Hang on a minute, what about the farm? We can't just up and leave in the middle of the herb season,' said Craig, looking at his wife and recognising with alarm that she was rubbing her chin, which meant she was actually considering this crazy idea. 'We have to prune the citrus trees, and what about the goats? You're not serious, surely?'

'The campdraft isn't until March. The herb season will be over,' Jess said quickly, 'and we could do the pruning early. I'll help in my spare time.'

Craig raised one eyebrow at her. 'And the goats?'

'Won't they be okay turned out for a week?'

'What about the milkers?'

'There aren't any,' said Caroline. 'You know they're all dry at the moment. Actually, it would be a really good time to get away.'

'Yippee! We're going!'

Jess jumped up and threw her arms around her father's neck. He only ever did the one-eyebrow trick when he was in a good mood. Craig braced himself and raised his half-full coffee cup in the air so as not to spill it.

'No promises, Jess. We'd have to think about it properly and organise some things. Maybe we can go. And I mean *maybe*.'

Jess smothered him with kisses.

'Oh, good grief!' Craig gasped for air. 'Stop slobbering on me, will you?'

'Come on. Let's go and plant those mulga seeds before it gets too hot,' suggested Caroline. 'Then we'll cook up a fine draftcamping breakfast.'

'That's campdrafting, Mum,' said Jess, walking to the door and pulling her new hat down on her head.

'Campdrafting. A good *campdrafting* breakfast. Those cows had better look out!'

'Hang on a minute! We haven't decided yet,' called Craig from the lounge room.

'Oh, give it up, Dad,' called Jess. 'You know you're outnumbered!'

Jess and Caroline made their way out to the garden. The ground was still lumpy over Diamond's grave, but tiny shoots of green had begun to poke up through the dirt. Caroline took a rake. 'We'll just loosen the soil so those seeds can get a better grip on life, Jess.'

Jess carefully emptied the contents of the packet into the palm of her hand and then poked her finger into the ground, making little holes and placing the seeds in one by one. When they had pressed them all in and watered them, Caroline headed back to the house. 'I'll come up in a minute,' called Jess, sitting down under Diamond's tree. She ran her hand over the ground. 'I'll do this somehow, Diamond,' she whispered. 'I'll win the money and buy Walkabout and it'll be like old times again.'

16

THE NEXT DAY, Dodger trotted up to the fence for his morning feed. He had put on condition and his coat looked a bit healthier, but he still had a big saggy belly. The resentment Jess once felt for him had waned since she had last handled him, but he still didn't seem like *her* horse. She climbed through the fence and Dodger snorted with surprise. He didn't usually get so much as a 'hello'.

While he was eating his hay, she gave him a good brush and combed out his tail. His feet were a bit overgrown and he would need shoes, but to start with she could work him in the arena, where it was soft underfoot. The gear she had put together last time she rode him was still in the tackroom and, once he finished eating, she saddled him up without incident and led him down to Harry's.

At Harry's she tied him up to the hitching rail alongside the other horses. He stood there with his lower lip hanging out, looking like an absolute train wreck next to the long-legged, gleaming colts, Legsy and Nosey. Tom, Luke, Grace and Rosie gathered around waiting for Harry's appraisal.

Jess cringed. It was ridiculous. Dodger wasn't going to win any campdrafts. Why was she even doing this?

Harry limped over and gave Dodger a rub under his thick forelock. 'Geez, he's got a head like a beaten favourite,' he chuckled. 'How old is he?' He pushed open Dodger's mouth and had a quick look at his teeth. Then he ran his hand down the horse's neck and over his shoulder. 'Station-bred, by the looks of this brand.'

Harry talked away as he passed his hands over Dodger, picking up the horse's feet and looking at his hooves, inspecting every bump on his legs with an experienced thumb. 'These old legs could tell a few stories,' he said. 'He seems sound enough, though.' He moved around the tail end and all the way along Dodger's back. 'A horse for all the family, they'd call him out west,' he said. 'Long in the back, isn't he?'

Harry approached the other shoulder. 'Well, I'll be jiggered!' he said in astonishment. 'He's got the same stud brand as old Bunyip.' He ran a couple of fingers over the three horizontal bars on the Dodger's shoulder and his expression changed.

He grinned at Jess and she saw something come alive

in his eyes. 'If he comes from Triple Bar stud, he's going to be a half-handy pony, I give you the tip,' he said. His blue eyes twinkled. 'Not many horses like this around now.'

'Really?' said Jess, shocked at such a positive assessment. 'But don't you think he's a bit . . .'

'He's a bit of a roughie, but so was old Bunyip. You don't need a show pony to bring in the cattle. These station-bred horses are as hardy as they come; honest too. I bet he has plenty of cattle sense.'

Harry ran his hands over Dodger's wither and gave it a gentle squeeze. Dodger quivered violently and arched his back. He put his ears back and screwed up his nose. But before Jess could call him crazy again, Harry said, 'You a bit sore there, old fella?' He fingered a patch of white hair on the horse's shoulder and then turned to Jess. 'Where's your saddle, kiddo?'

Jess pointed to the saddle on the fence rail.

'Is that the one you rode him in when you had the accident?'

'Yes . . . ?'

'Pony-club saddle,' he grunted with disdain. 'Be a love and get me a bottle of talcum powder out of the cupboard in the tackroom, will you?'

When Jess gave him the powder, Harry took the saddle and turned it upside down. There were two long panels, designed to sit either side of the horse's spine. Harry gave them a sprinkle. Then he slung the saddle onto Dodger's back, gave it a few pats and took it off again, leaving patches of white dust on the horse's back.

'Come and have a look at this,' he said. 'See how the powder came off on his shoulder and it's in patches along his back? It should leave one long mark, to show that the pressure is evenly distributed. These white hairs on his shoulder are where the saddle was pinching him. That would explain why he's been tossing his head around.'

'But it never gave Diamond any problems,' said Jess.

'Was she fifteen hands high with a broad wither?'

'No, she was . . .'

'About thirteen hands high with a narrow wither?'

'Um, yeah.' Jess felt really stupid.

Harry gave her a friendly wink. 'Told you there was no such thing as a dumb horse.'

Jess patted Dodger on the neck. 'I'm so sorry, Dodger.'

'Let's get a proper stock saddle on him,' said Harry. 'Dunno how you can sit in them self-unloaders anyway.'

He shuffled into the tackroom and came out a moment later with a big old stock saddle. 'This oughta fit a bit better,' he said, slinging it over Dodger's back. After checking the fit, he said, 'Righto, let's see what this old brumby can do.' He led him over to the round yard.

Shutting the gate behind him, Harry slapped Dodger on the rump and let him go free. The horse settled into a steady rhythm, trotting like clockwork around the edge of the circular yard.

Harry stood in the centre and grinned. 'I reckon he's been in a yard or two.' Then he stepped out into the pathway of the horse.

As if anticipating this move, Dodger spun around and trotted off in the other direction, immediately settling back into a steady tempo. He locked one of his long ears in Harry's direction, ready for the next signal. Harry slapped his hands on his thighs in delight. 'Yep, he can get about all right. Watch this!'

He stepped in front of the horse again. Like lightning, Dodger spun on his heel and settled back into a rhythm as if nothing had happened. Harry repeated the same move a few more times and then clicked his tongue, urging the horse up into a canter. From a faster gait, Dodger spun and turned effortlessly. After a few minutes he put his nose to the ground, and a long, resigned sigh spluttered from his nostrils.

'Whoa, old fella,' Harry called. Dodger immediately came back to a walk and turned towards Harry. Harry gave him a rub on the forehead. 'Good man.' He walked to the gate and Dodger followed like a shadow. 'Got your helmet, Jess?'

'She can use mine!' Grace called out, unbuckling her chinstrap and holding it out eagerly.

Jess instantly felt panicky. Dodger spun so fast – what if she couldn't keep up with him? What if she came off in front of everyone? What if . . .

'Here you go, Jessy.' Grace pushed the helmet into her lap.

'Thanks.' Jess turned it over in her hands and inspected the inside, stalling for time. It had 'Australian Safety Standard Approved' written on the inner label.

'What, do you reckon I've got nits or something?' grinned Grace. She took the helmet back and lifted it to Jess's head. 'Come on, you'll be okay.'

Jess dodged the helmet and grappled it out of Grace's hands. 'Okay, okay. I'm putting it on. Give me half a chance.' She stepped back to give herself a bit of elbow room, placed the helmet on her head and fiddled with the chinstrap.

The helmet was a perfect fit. It felt good and snug. 'Now all I need is a padded suit,' Jess mumbled as she stepped towards Dodger. Harry stood patiently, holding him by the reins.

'Harry won't let anything happen to you,' said Grace. 'He'd never put you up there if it wasn't safe.'

Harry gave her a warm smile. 'You'll be fine, Jess,' he said, as he handed her the reins. 'He's a good horse.'

Jess set her jaw hard and stared Dodger in the eye, determined to get control of her nerves. Dodger rolled an eyeball and stiffened his back. She flipped a rein over his neck, getting ready to mount, then took a large chunk of his thick mane in her hand. She had to do this. She had to get through it. Dodger raised his head and arched his neck.

She felt a hand on her shoulder.

'Why don't you just give him a pat for a minute?' Harry stepped around her and took the reins back over Dodger's neck. 'Just give yourself some time to say hello to him.'

He gently pried Jess's hand from the mane and placed it on Dodger's shoulder. 'There you go,' he said in his rusty voice. 'Give the old fella a pat first.' He let go and took a step back.

Jess dropped her hand. 'I just don't trust him,' she said, feeling bitter disappointment. She wanted to cry. Dodger took a step away from her. 'Look, he just doesn't like me. He's fine around everyone else.'

Luke came forward. He ran a calm hand over the old stockhorse's nose and Dodger visibly melted. 'You can trust him, Jess,' he said in a quiet voice. 'If you don't hurt him, he won't hurt you.'

'But I've never hurt him,' said Jess.

'They know everything you're thinking. They just mirror what you do.'

Jess watched the way Dodger was pushing his forehead into Luke's hand like a kitten. She could almost hear him purring.

Her head told her she could do this. She could make Diamond purr. She'd made friends with Wally. But her heart . . .

Pretend he's Diamond.

Jess took the reins from Luke and began to pat Dodger's neck. She closed her eyes. He felt smooth and warm. He smelled great. She ran her hand up and over his ears and along the top of his neck, and felt him relax a little. She kept scratching just behind the ears, until he pushed into her hand and snorted softly. She smiled – he was like a different horse.

Jess spent a bit more time running her hands over his face and scratching his cheeks. She rubbed his forehead and tickled under his chin. Dodger went all gooey and waggled his top lip. After several more minutes, she turned to Luke. 'I think I'm ready to get on him now.'

Luke nodded.

She ran her hand over Dodger a few more times, flipped the reins over his neck and took hold of a stirrup. This time it felt routine. It felt right. She was ready, he was ready.

Jess gave a quick hop and hoisted herself up and Dodger stood quietly while she eased herself into the stock saddle. It was like an armchair, immediately making her feel relaxed. She gathered up her reins, leaned forward and gave him a pat on the neck. 'Okay, boy. Let's try this again.'

She gave Dodger a gentle squeeze with her legs, keeping her face well up. He walked off without fuss.

'Feel okay?' Harry asked.

'So far,' Jess answered. She walked him around a couple of laps and then eased him into a trot. His stride was smooth and rhythmic and soon she was cantering around the big arena. Dodger had a long, loping stride that was easy to sit to. It was amazing what a difference the new saddle made.

She hadn't realised how much she had missed riding.

She cantered Dodger in big circles, changing direction every now and then to form figure eights. Tom and Luke hung their arms over the top rail and watched. Rosie and Grace climbed up onto the fence.

'Go, Jess!' Grace called out, ecstatic that Jess was back in the saddle.

Jess laughed and held up a thumb. 'I'm going, I'm going.'

Harry shuffled out into the arena and began tinkering with something in the corner. Along the side fence were two ropes running the length of the arena, one above the other. At one end the rope wound around a large bicycle wheel and back along the fence. At the other end, it went around what looked like the back end of the bicycle.

Harry tied a chaff bag to the top rope so that it dangled from the middle. Then he clambered onto the end post and began to pedal the bicycle. The rope ran around the wheels, sending the chaff bag back and forth along the arena. It was quite a contraption.

'What on earth is that?' Jess asked.

'It's Harry's cow-cycle,' said Rosie. 'That's how we teach a horse to follow a cow. They learn to lock onto something and follow it back and forth. The rider can also practise giving the horse the correct signals.'

'Righto, let's put him on the bag,' said Harry. 'Bring him over for a look, Jess.'

Jess rode Dodger over to the crazy contraption, wondering how this would pan out.

'Let him have a sniff,' said Harry.

Dodger held out his neck and gave a soft snort at the bag. As he was sniffing it, Harry pedalled the rope, taking the bag a small distance from the horse's nose. Dodger propped both ears forward and followed it. The bag stopped and Dodger stopped. Harry pedalled again and Dodger walked along, following it.

'Hold on, Jess,' Harry called out as he back-pedalled, sending the bag in the opposite direction.

Dodger spun on his heels, nearly tipping Jess off. She grabbed for the front of the saddle and hung on as he followed the bag up the arena.

'And again,' Harry called out. This time Jess sat into the saddle, anticipating the spin as Harry sent Dodger back the other way.

'Stick your legs forward and loosen your waist, Jess,' Tom called out.

'Get your heels down,' shouted Rosie.

Grace yelled, 'Take it in the guts, Jessy!'

Jess tried to follow all the instructions being hurled at her.

After a few more turns, she and Dodger were effortlessly following the bag up and down the arena. Harry kept it slow until Jess got the feel for it, and then he began to crank it up.

'You get over here and pedal. I'm too old for this caper,' Harry wheezed, motioning to Luke.

Luke climbed up onto the post and took over the pedals. The bag went sailing up the arena, coaxing Dodger into a short gallop – then, without warning, bag and horse changed direction, leaving Jess desperately clinging on. Just as she found her seat, Dodger spun again and galloped the other way. Left, right, left, right: Jess sank into the saddle and took each turn in her waist, gaining a rhythm with Dodger, who crouched down and darted back and forth.

'He's a little ripper!' yelled Harry gleefully.

Tom and the girls clapped and hooted loudly. Luke sat

on the post, grinning. The horse was a magician.

As Jess walked Dodger around to cool him off she couldn't get the smile off her face. She couldn't wait to have a go at cutting some real cattle. Dodger had a secret past that she didn't think Hetty even knew about. He must have been an absolute star in his day.

As she led Dodger out the front gate later that afternoon, she took a moment to look him over. He was scruffy, that was for sure, and his feet . . .

His feet were neatly trimmed!

Jess looked up and saw Luke by the yard putting a bucket of tools away.

'Thanks, Luke,' she called out. He looked up, nodded, and kept walking.

He's nice.

On her way home, Jess wondered what sort of a life Dodger had had. He wasn't a young horse; his muzzle was grey and his teeth were long. He must be in his twenties. She wondered how many owners he'd had and what other talents he might be hiding. She thought of Black Beauty, in her favourite storybook, and how many different owners he'd been through – some kind, some cruel.

She gave Dodger a slap on the neck. 'This is going to be a kind chapter in your life, Dodger, I promise.'

17

WHEN JESS TURNED UP at Rosie and Grace's place for the first time, she wondered if she had the right place. She'd expected a well-tended stud farm, but the Arnold house was surrounded by junk. There were crooked piles of old bricks, tangled steel, old engines and slabs of timber, all cluttered along the muddy, potholed driveway. There was just enough room for a vehicle to grind its way through.

Among the debris, an assortment of horses chewed on their morning feed. She recognised Buster, who stood out from the rest in a clean blue rug and a clean blue halter, eating out of a clean blue feed bin.

Fat red chooks waddled between the horses' legs, pecking at the morsels of grain that fell from their mouths. As Jess rode up the driveway, the sour-sweet smells of manure in mud and hot, moist lucerne hung heavily in the still air. It was a smell that, before the rain, would have been quite delicious. But now, only hours later, it had a slightly decomposing edge that didn't travel up the nostrils quite so smoothly.

There was a sudden frenzy of squawking and barking as a black kelpie chased a chook across the front yard. A woman brandishing a stick marched after them in old gumboots, wearing jeans and a baseball cap with black hair sticking out in all directions from under it. She was Grace and Rosie's mum – Mrs Arnold. Jess recognised her from gymkhanas. She had the Blake nose. She was Harry's sister; Lawson's aunt.

Jess sat there on her horse, feeling awkward, as Mrs Arnold caught up with the dog and unleashed a string of colourful expletives. The dog spat out a mouthful of red feathers and darted off under an old tractor with its tail between its legs.

'*Stanley!*' Mrs Arnold shrieked. 'Come and get this mongrel dog of yours before I shoot it!'

Yep, they're related all right – gun freaks the lot of them!

Mr Arnold, who Jess had also seen at gymkhanas, walked onto the verandah, leaving the front door to bang behind him. He grumbled something and pulled on some Cuban-heeled boots.

Rosie and Grace appeared from under the house in oilskin jackets, each carrying a saddle.

'Mum's in a bad mood,' whispered Rosie to Jess.

'Yeah, let's get out of here,' said Grace.

Jess rode beside the girls as they walked down a dirt track that led to a large paddock by the river flats. 'Where are Tom and Luke?' she asked.

'Luke's saddling up Muscles, our stallion. Dad said he could ride him. Tom's riding along the river flats. They'll meet us down the paddock.' Grace glanced back over her shoulder and said, 'Poor Dad.' Then she changed the subject. 'We taught Handbrake to steer without any reins. I'll show you when I catch her.'

'Which one is Handbrake?' Jess asked. She couldn't keep up with all the different horses Grace rode.

'She's the bay filly we got from the saleyards. Dad called her Handbrake because she's so lazy. He wants me to draft her and sell her on as a kids' horse.'

As they walked down to a big grazing paddock, horses and cattle were scattered about the flats. The air smelt much better down there among the trees and pasture.

Grace went off in search of Handbrake, while Buster nudged a carrot out of Rosie's hand. As the girls readied their horses, a long, sharp whistle sounded behind them. Jess turned to see Luke riding Muscles, who whinnied and grunted to the mares. The disgraced chicken-killer trotted along behind.

The stallion was a deep liver colour that changed whenever the sun caught him at a different angle. One minute he looked chocolate brown and the next he was golden, or copper, or red. Jess had never seen such a coat.

She gazed over the mix of cattle. They were all shapes and sizes, from big old Friesians to runty black heifers and brindled Brahmans. 'Are they the ones we're going to practise on?'

'Well, technically, yes,' said Rosie. She gave Jess a cheeky smile. 'But we gotta go get our bull out of the neighbour's paddock first and that might involve a bit of, er, reshuffling of some cattle.' She lowered her voice to a whisper and moved closer to Jess. 'Why stir up our cattle when we can stir up the neighbour's, hey?'

'Napoleon keeps jumping the fence,' said Grace. 'He's in Mr Donaldson's paddocks again. The old fella will have a stroke if he finds him in there again.'

'It'll be good practice for you to draft him out, Jess,' said Rosie.

'Hey, look, here comes Tom!' said Luke. He put his fingers to his mouth and let out another whistle. Tom waved as he cantered up on a jet-black colt.

The group headed down along the river flats towards a gate that separated the over-grazed Arnold property from the noticeably lusher pasture of Mr Donaldson's. A neat herd of plump red and white Herefords grazed alongside a huge white bull.

'Lucky Mr Donaldson has gone into town for a few

weeks, so he won't know Napoleon got in again,' Rosie said, swinging the gate open. 'He spends a fortune on Hereford semen. He totally freaks if he finds our Brahman bull in here.'

'Dad reckons we should charge old Donaldson stud fees for using our bull like that,' said Grace giggled. 'All those quality Brafords he gets each year.'

'So, we're only down here to get the bull back in, aren't we?' said Luke.

'Yes, of course we are,' said Rosie, nudging Buster into a trot. 'We just have to move the other cattle a bit so we can get to him.'

The group spread out around the animals, quietly bringing them to a closely packed mob at the end of the paddock. While the girls held them in a group, Luke singled out one beast, moved it away and began to work it, making it look easy. Then Grace and Rosie had a go. Jess was amazed at how quick and agile such big, clumpy beasts could be.

'Your turn,' said Grace, pulling up her mare and giving her a pat.

Jess eyed the mob that Luke and Rosie held in the corner of the paddock. Dodger stepped up his pace and pricked his ears when he realised they were headed for the cattle. He felt like a coiled spring beneath her, bouncing from one leg to another. She held him steady.

'Find one with a doe eye,' said Luke. 'One that looks a bit quiet.'

Jess looked at the twenty or so cattle. They all looked the same to her: scatty and nervous. Then she spied a small steer with what she thought might be a placid expression. She slipped Dodger between it and the mob as she had seen Luke do, and to her delight it moved away. But it just as quickly ducked under Dodger's neck and scuttled back to the mob. She chased it too late and scattered the cattle in all directions. She tried again, only to have the same thing happen.

Luke rode over to her. 'Keep the horse's shoulder to the beast and rein him back one step before you turn him. That'll sit him on his hindquarters and he'll spin better.'

'Okay.'

She set off towards the mob to try again.

'Pick Napoleon this time,' Luke called out.

Jess looked at the huge grey bull. He was twice the size of Dodger and had two seriously pointy horns jutting out of his head. From his chest came a deep, rumbling bellow.

He had to be kidding!

She looked back at Luke, expecting to see a grin, but he just shrugged. 'We have to get him sometime. See if you can bring him back to the gate.'

Jess approached Napoleon, unable to take her eyes off

149

his deadly-looking horns. To her relief, he swished his tail and walked in the other direction. She placed herself between the bull and the others. As he tried to return to the mob, she reined Dodger back onto his hind leg and to her complete surprise he spun effortlessly to block Napoleon.

Napoleon moseyed back and forth a few times in a half-hearted fashion, pointing his enormous horns directly at her, but Dodger danced in tandem and forced him back each time.

Cool fun! I am queen of the cattle yard!

'Bring him to the gate,' yelled Rosie.

Jess directed the bull towards the gate and to her delight he did as he was told, walking obediently away from the herd. Her confidence soared. She couldn't wait to have a go at something a bit faster.

They spent the afternoon cantering around after the cattle, and Jess steadily got the hang of things.

'Get up on its shoulder!' Grace yelled out. 'Stay clear of its hind legs. Push it around!'

'*Hah!*' Jess yelled. She held the reins up Dodger's neck, urging him on faster as he galloped up onto a steer's shoulder. With ears flat back, her horse leaned heavily into the beast and physically shoved it around a makeshift peg.

When Jess finally pulled up, her cheeks were flushed

bright red and her smile was huge. She loosened the reins and walked the puffing horse to the sidelines. She had never felt so exhilarated. Dodger was an absolute genius on cattle.

'He's a great horse,' said Luke, riding alongside her. 'You're gonna do all right at that draft, I reckon.'

'Thanks!' said Jess.

He held her gaze for a moment, then grinned and looked away.

Grace rode up next to Jess and reached over to pat Dodger on the neck. 'What a good boy! You could teach Handbrake here a few lessons, couldn't you?' She gave her own horse a pat. 'I think it's the breeding paddock for you, girlie.'

Handbrake raised her head suddenly, stared towards the river and let out a long whinny. They all followed her stare and saw two helmets bobbing through the trees. A white horse glistened in the sun and Jess could see the motion of a crop on the other horse's rump, *tap, tap* with every stride.

'I can't *stand* those girls,' said Grace.

'You hate everyone,' said Rosie.

'They'll dob on us for sure,' said Jess.

'It'll be okay,' said Rosie. 'We were just getting our bull back. I'll explain everything to Dad and he'll talk to Mr Donaldson. It'll be fine, you'll see.'

Jess rode home that evening feeling hopeful and determined. She would win that money and save Walkabout from a dreadful future. She leaned forward to give Dodger a pat. What good luck he'd turned out to be.

Her father was waiting, arms folded, as she turned Dodger into the driveway. 'Do you mind telling me where you've been riding today, Jess?'

'We've been practising drafting, Dad. Dodger is going so well. Everyone's really impressed with him.' Jess gave the horse a slap on the neck. 'Aren't they, old boy?'

'So Mr Donaldson tells me,' said Craig, a thunderous look on his face. 'He just rang all the way from the city to tell me you've been stirring up his prize Herefords.'

Jess pulled Dodger to a halt and jumped out of the saddle.

'Mr Arnold's bull got into his paddock and we had to get it out. We just had a bit of a play with the steers, but we didn't go near the breeding stock,' she explained.

'Well, Mr Donaldson tells me you *were* chasing the breeding stock,' said Craig.

'What? That's not true! Who told him that?' she said, knowing full well who had.

That pair of poo-magnets.

'It doesn't matter who told him. You shouldn't have been in his paddocks,' said Craig. 'How would you like someone coming into your paddock and chasing your horse around while you weren't home? You'd be livid. It's trespassing. It's wrong.'

'But we were getting Mr Arnold's bull out of there. He asked us to,' argued Jess.

That didn't seem to placate her father one bit.

'Who is this Mr Arnold? Isn't he the one who is supposed to be taking you all the way to Longwood for a horse show?' said Craig, his voice getting louder. 'What sort of responsible adult is he?'

'He *is* responsible, Dad. Rosie said he will talk to Mr Donaldson and explain. He'll be grateful that we got the bull out.'

'I spoke to Mr Donaldson and he wasn't grateful at all. He was very annoyed.'

'Only because those two evil witches lied and said we were chasing the breeding stock. Mr Arnold—'

Craig cut her off. 'Mr Arnold should have spoken to Mr Donaldson *before* he sent you down there to chase those cattle. I don't know about you going off to Longwood with these people, Jessica. I don't like you going off for miles with people we hardly know, and besides, you've already got a horse. Now put Dodger away and get your tail up to the house.'

Jess was horrified. 'But I *have* to go to Longwood, so I can buy Wally,' she said, running after her father and leading Dodger behind her. 'Dad, Mr Arnold is going to talk to Mr Donaldson. It'll all get sorted out, you'll see. Katrina and Tegan are just trying to get us in trouble.'

'Just because a person seems nice doesn't mean they're responsible,' he said. 'I've heard some pretty crazy stories about those Arnolds, Jess, and they don't sound like the sort of people you'd want to pin your hopes and dreams on. Apparently the wife is a total eccentric.'

'She's not coming.'

Craig shook his head. 'I don't know, Jess. I'm concerned about this whole new scene you've become involved in. I barely see you these days. Your mother and I will have to think about it. Meanwhile, you're not to ride until you've apologised to Mr Donaldson.' He began to walk up the front steps.

'But he's away in the city!'

'Well, you'll just have to wait until he comes back. You'll be starting school on Monday, which is a lot more important than riding horses and chasing people's cattle. I think you should be focusing on that, don't you?'

'But it's the last few days of the holidays!'

'Today is Thursday. It won't kill you to spend three days at home, Jessica,' said Craig, walking through the doorway.

'Da-a-ad! Can't I even go over to Harry's?' Jess called out after him.

'No!' he yelled back.

18

'CAN'T I GO and see Walkabout this afternoon?' Jess whined. She had been trying on uniforms, picking up books, sorting out her old wardrobe and spring-cleaning her room. She hadn't ridden Dodger or seen her new friends for three days, and it was sending her crazy.

'No, darling, your father has grounded you until you apologise to Mr Donaldson,' her mother answered.

'But that is so unfair!' cried Jess. 'Katrina and Tegan made up a pack of lies. As soon as Donaldson gets back and Mr Arnold talks to him, you'll understand, and I'll have been grounded for nothing.'

'You have not been grounded for nothing,' said Caroline firmly. 'You were chasing his cattle without permission. Breeding stock or no breeding stock, you were trespassing.'

'Why can't I just apologise over the phone? What if

Mr Donaldson decides not to come back from the city this weekend?'

'Jessica, you are to apologise in person. That is the decent thing to do.'

Jess sulked. 'Am I at least allowed to exercise Dodger on a lunge rope? He'll lose all his fitness otherwise.'

'In one week?'

'Yes, it's only six weeks until the campdraft and he's badly out of shape. I need all the time I can get or he won't be fit enough. And what about me? I can't afford to lose a whole week of training, Mum.'

'Oh, okay. You can lunge him, but don't you dare get on him,' said Caroline.

Jess breathed a sigh of relief. 'Thanks, Mum.'

She grabbed a drink and went and sat by the old coachwood tree to speak to Diamond. 'Dodger is going to help save Walkabout, Dimey, so it is very important that we look after him,' she explained to the patch of mulga seedlings. 'So, I might have to let him stay in your stable.' She knew Diamond would understand. Actually, since getting to know Dodger, Jess had become sure that the two horses would have been quite good friends.

After clearing it with Diamond, she decided to freshen up the lean-to for Dodger. First, she hauled out the old straw and spread it around the veggie patch. Then she pulled out three new bales of straw and fluffed them around. When the stall was perfect, she set about cleaning up the old stock saddle that Harry had lent her. She went over all the stitching with a toothbrush, polished the brass buckles and rubbed its fenders down with glycerine soap. Then, when she had removed the teeniest speck of dirt and grime, she went over it with leather dressing until it was flopsy and supple.

She took Dodger out into the big paddock on a long lunge rope and he trotted and cantered around her, grateful for the company. He soon picked up on her voice commands and she found she could send him over logs and other small jumps. He jumped off the old loading ramp and ran up and down gullies.

When she brought him back to the yard, she spent hours grooming him, giggling at how he waggled his top lip when she rubbed at an itchy spot. He followed her around the yard nibbling at her back pockets while she filled water buckets and picked up poo. One morning when she went down to his stall early, she found him lying down with his legs curled under him and she knelt down next to him and scratched behind his ears. He closed his eyes again and after a few minutes began to snore. Jess had never heard a horse snore before and Dodger woke with a start when she burst out laughing.

But as Monday got closer, no amount of time with

Dodger could distract her from thinking about Shara. Would she be there at school, or would she be starting at Canningdale College?

Despite being forewarned, Jess was stunned to find there was no Shara. She had been accepted into the selective high school.

Jess was flattened. Everyone at school but her seemed to already know. Katrina Pettilow told her, in a smirky voice, and called her *Nigel-no-mates*. Jess wanted to slap her. Twice. Once for the nasty name and a second time for being a dobber. She wished she could go to Rosie and Grace's school in the neighbouring district. There were heaps more horsey girls in that school. Most of the girls in Jess's class were surfers or emos, except for Katrina and Tegan. She found it hard to talk to them, even though most of them were friendly enough.

She spent all week lying low and trying to concoct a genuine-sounding apology for Mr Donaldson. At home, she tried to win brownie points by helping with the washing, doing the dishes at the first request rather than the fifth, and by cleaning the bathroom and toilet unasked. She was willing to lower herself to any level to get to that draft. But every time she asked if she was allowed to go,

Craig said, 'I haven't decided yet.' He was milking her for all the housework he could get, she was sure.

Friday finally came and Craig drove her to Mr Donaldson's farm after school. She had never met him before and wasn't at all sure what to expect. As it turned out, he was in his nineties and seemed confused about exactly who she was and why she was talking about his cattle. When the conversation became a labyrinth of twisted and confused communication, Jess figured she'd done her bit and left him scratching his head outside his front door. She ran back down the driveway to her father, who was waiting in the car.

'Manage to redeem yourself?' asked Craig in a stern voice.

Jess pulled a confused face and put her arms in the air. 'Who knows? He's a day older than God. I couldn't understand a word he said!'

Craig looked concerned.

Jess backtracked quickly. 'Yes! Yes! He's cool with everything! He's fine – I told you he would be!'

Her dad seemed to relax a little.

'Can I have a lift down to Harry's place now?' She was absolutely busting to see Wally and catch up with her friends.

'Yes, I want to meet these people and find out more about this campdraft,' answered her father.

Craig introduced himself to Harry and, like Jess, was made to feel instantly welcome. There was much hand-shaking and nodding and talk about tractors and rain. When Harry discovered Craig was a tree-changing ex-accountant and Craig found out Harry was a retired diesel mechanic, they soon realised there was some handy bartering to be done.

'He's a sensible bloke,' Craig commented in the car on the way home. 'Seems to know a bit about tractors. He's going to have a go at fixing the PTO on ours. I'll help him with his books in return.' He looked chuffed.

'Is he sensible enough to take me to the draft?' asked Jess.

Craig cuffed her on the head. 'Well, what sort of a dad would I be if I didn't let you at least have a shot at it?'

19

SCHOOL WASN'T TOO BAD, even without Shara's close friendship. Jess found her biology classes quite interesting, and was thrilled when her teacher let her choose horse genetics as her topic for the major project.

Katrina Pettilow chose the same topic. 'I need to study up on genetics for when I go to Canningdale College,' Jess overheard her telling Tegan in the library. 'It's very relevant to the animal science I'll be studying there.'

'In your dreams,' Jess muttered as she walked past.

Katrina looked up and glared at her. 'Luckily *my* parents can afford to send me and I won't have to *beg* my way in like some people.'

'Winning a scholarship is hardly begging,' said Jess, assuming she was talking about Shara. 'And anyway, it's still selective.'

And who'd select you?

'Defending her now, are you?' Katrina retorted.

Jess refused to bite. 'Why aren't you there now if you're so cashed up?'

'They don't start vet science till Year Ten, *der*,' said Katrina, 'and then, who knows, maybe I'll make a new best friend there!'

Jess burst out laughing. 'I doubt it.' The idea of Katrina and Shara getting chummy was ludicrous.

For the next few weeks, Jess was driven to study hard and get a higher mark than Katrina. She got lost for hours on the internet reading about different spotting genes in Appaloosa horses. Her new-found study ethic seemed to earn good brownie points with her dad and Jess came to a good working arrangement with him. She could keep Dodger at Harry's place and train for the campdraft after school if she promised to do her homework first thing in the morning. She found it much easier to wake up early and focus on her studies when she knew that Dodger had been trained the evening before.

In the afternoons, she would jump off the school bus near Harry's place. Tom was often on the same bus, and they would run down to Harry's together. Once there, she would usually find Luke closing a gate behind a yard of cattle. Grace and Rosie would be in the tackroom, ripping off their school uniforms and wriggling into their jeans.

Katrina would often float around the arena on Chelpie, looking like Princess Perfect, but she rarely had a go at drafting. When she did, it was disastrous. Chelpie rushed at the cattle with her ears flat back and bit them. In the yard, the little mare became so aggressive that the cows nearly jumped out of it. Tegan's pony was frightened of the cattle and way too small to be campdrafting. Harry quickly banned both of them from working any cattle. Jess couldn't imagine how either of them would ever ride in the draft.

Craig came to pick her up from Harry's each afternoon and often turned up early. Jess loved having him watch her ride Dodger for a while before they drove home. He constantly told her how proud he was of her and how well she was riding, but she sensed that he still doubted her chances of winning. Jess couldn't wait to show him how Dodger handled cattle. He'd soon change his thinking.

A week before the draft, she got her opportunity. Harry invited her to a special practice session at his place. As was the way with campdrafting, many hands were needed to bring in the cattle and to work the gates, so unfortunately, this included not just Lawson, but Katrina and Tegan as well, who Harry had promised could try chasing cattle under more controlled conditions.

On the night, Jess cantered Dodger under the flood-lights. The darkness made big black curtains around the arena, and it was weird riding with the sound of crickets chirruping in the background.

Dodger was now a ball of muscle. Jess had clipped off his mane and combed out his shaggy forelock, giving him what she thought was a rather noble appearance. The masculine look suited him. In any case, she was learning that a pretty horse had little standing in the world of campdrafting. It was all about performance – spins, sliding stops, rollbacks and lead changes, and above all else, cow sense. She reined Dodger to a stop and then trotted him on again to get his full attention.

Nearby, Lawson cantered on a thickset chestnut gelding, spinning it in tight circles and then spurring it off in the other direction. Jess couldn't help noticing that he occasionally glanced at her. When he did, she spun away, not wanting to look at him. He gave her the creeps.

Grace and Rosie were in the yards with the cattle. She could see her father with Harry and Stanley Arnold, each sitting on a bucket. Harry chewed his toothpick, Stanley turned his hat around in his hands and Craig sipped from a thermos of hot coffee.

They all stared in her direction, and she did a quick rollback.

Her dad was talking about her, Jess was sure, asking them if she had any chance of winning the draft. She'd show him!

As she changed direction, she nearly ran into Lawson. He walked his horse straight at her and held up a hand.

'Jessica Fairley, isn't it?'

She spun away, pretending not to hear him. Creep!

Lawson followed her. 'You're that kid who was down on the river flats.'

Jess rode on. Now Lawson was really weirding her out.

'It wasn't you, okay,' he said, pulling his horse to a halt.

'Leave me alone,' said Jess, pushing Dodger into a canter. She had no idea what he was talking about and she wasn't interested.

To her relief, Lawson shrugged, rode away to the other end of the arena and continued working his horse. Jess brought Dodger back to a walk and gave him a rest for a while.

Katrina entered the arena. She began working Chelpie in a collected walk, and quickly progressed to shoulder-in and half-pass. Breaking into a canter, Chelpie began circling the arena like a little white rocking horse. Katrina looked completely faultless, sitting beautifully in the saddle and riding with gloved hands and an elegant dressage whip. Jess became grudgingly mesmerised.

As Katrina passed Lawson, Chelpie let fly with a hind leg, lashing out at Lawson's horse. The movement was so quick and agile that Chelpie barely broke her rhythm, but the gelding lurched sideways and nearly tipped Lawson out of the saddle.

Caught by surprise, Lawson gathered the reins and gave his horse a kick in the ribs. 'Cut it out,' he growled.

Lawson kept cantering his horse around the edge of the arena. Chelpie cantered past without missing a beat. Then Katrina changed direction and cantered up behind him. Chelpie lunged at his horse's rump with her teeth bared. The gelding clamped its tail down and skittled sideways.

This time Lawson did notice. He spun around and glared at Katrina. 'You wanna get a bloody handle on that horse.'

Katrina scowled at him, brought Chelpie under control and pushed her back into a canter.

Lawson continued working his gelding. White froth dripped from its mouth and its nostrils blew hard. Jess noticed him glance over at the other men periodically. When he realised he had their attention, he spun the horse at the far end of the arena and pushed it into a gallop back up the long side. As he neared the fence, he slammed on the skids so hard that the gelding's hooves sent gravel and stones spraying through the fence at Harry, Stanley and Craig. They jumped back and screened their faces with their arms.

'Lawson!' yelled Harry. 'What are you doing?'

Lawson sat on the puffing horse and laughed. 'You blokes gonna sit there lolly-gagging like old women, or are you gonna come and move some cattle?'

He spun the horse on its heel and trotted off. As the gelding neared Chelpie, it started baulking. 'Get up,' he growled. He kicked his horse up and made it canter past.

Jess walked Dodger over to the fence near the men and watched on.

Whenever Chelpie went near Lawson's horse, it stopped and hunched its back, refusing to go forward.

'What's wrong with you today?' Lawson growled. He turned the horse around in a tight circle and then forced it to face up to Chelpie. The horse tried to escape by spinning sideways, but was blocked again by Lawson's pull on the reins and had no place left to go but up. It reared on its hind legs and paddled wildly with its front hooves.

Lawson was quick to respond, pulling heavily on the reins and setting his weight against the animal. It tumbled over backwards. Lawson jumped off and landed on his feet like a cat while the gelding came crashing down on its back, legs flailing in the air. As its head hit the ground, he leapt on its neck and pinned it down with one knee. It lay frozen, eyes rolling, nostrils blowing.

Harry's face hardened. Behind him a tall young man with red hair spoke. 'Well, that was impressive.'

Harry spun around. 'Geez, Ryan! What are you doing here?'

'Came to draft some cattle with you. Didn't think I'd see that, though,' Ryan said in a loud voice.

Lawson stepped off the horse's neck and let it struggle to its feet. 'You work your horses, Ryan, and I'll work mine.' He gathered his reins, put a foot in a stirrup and gave a couple of hops, ready to jump back into the saddle.

Ryan slid through the railings. 'Don't you think it's had enough?' he said to Lawson. 'Poor thing might collapse in front of everyone!'

'Get out of there, Ryan,' Harry called.

Ryan didn't seem to hear him. He grabbed the gelding by the bit.

Lawson put both feet back on the ground and turned to Ryan with a suddenly thunderous face. 'Get your hands off my horse,' he said through his teeth.

'Oh, give the poor thing a break,' said Ryan in a strangely jovial voice.

'I'll give *you* a break,' snarled Lawson, as he brushed Ryan's hand off the bit.

'Hey, come on, you two,' said Harry, standing up. 'Ryan, I've told you not to come around here when you've been drinking.'

Ryan took hold of the horse's bit again and stared Lawson in the eye. The gelding snorted and, sensing the tension between the two men, began dancing on the spot, wanting to get away.

'You heard what he said, back off,' said Lawson, squaring his shoulders and taking a step towards Ryan.

The gelding, no longer able to contain itself, pulled away, reefing the reins from both men and galloping to the other side of the arena.

'Or what?' said Ryan.

'Hey, come on, you blokes,' said Harry, raising his voice. 'If you two wanna carry on, then take it off my property.'

The two men took a step apart, but their eyes remained locked, neither willing to back down. Eventually, Ryan turned away and pulled himself through the fence. 'I'll leave you to your little party,' he said, dusting off his hat and giving his stepfather a nod.

Harry nodded but his eyes betrayed disappointment. He watched Ryan walk back to his truck.

'You wanna grab a coffee up at the house and make sure you're under the limit,' Harry called after him. 'You've got horses on board.'

Ryan waved a dismissive arm at him and slammed the door of his truck.

Jess walked Dodger over to the trembling gelding. 'Come on, fella,' she said softly, reaching for his reins. 'Come and walk with Dodger, he'll look after you.' She managed to get the reins over his head and lead him away.

Lawson marched towards Jess and held out his hands

for the reins. She promptly handed them over. Then she watched as Lawson left the arena, Ryan drove out the driveway, and Harry marched back to the house. She slumped in her saddle. The practice draft seemed over before it had begun.

'You're not going too, are you?' said a voice behind her. It was Luke.

'But Harry's gone. Everyone's leaving,' she said. 'What was that all about?'

'There's always trouble when Ryan comes home,' said Luke. 'I try to stay out of it.'

'Lawson is just so horrible.'

'Ryan's not the best, either.'

'So, are you one of their brothers too?' Jess asked, trying to work out this strange family.

'Lawson's Harry's son – he's blood. Ryan is Annie's son. Harry adopted him. And I'm fostered,' said Luke shortly. 'As long as we all remember who's top dog, there's usually no problem.'

Jess watched Lawson and his horse disappear into the stables. No doubt, he was the top dog.

'Come on,' Luke urged. 'Don't let them ruin it for us.'

'Do you think Harry will still take us to the draft?'

'Yeah, it'd take more than that to keep Harry away from a draft. Come on, I don't reckon he'll mind if we still work some cattle.'

'It'll be better without them here, anyway,' said Grace, riding past on Handbrake and letting herself into the yards.

Jess spent the evening perfecting her cut-out. Grace let a dozen or so cows into a large yard, which they called 'the camp'. Luke sat up on the rails and coached Jess, giving all sorts of advice about choosing a good beast, cutting it out from the mob and pushing it down towards the gates.

Tom stood behind the double gates and, when Jess had the beast cut and under control, he swung them open and let her out into the arena. He had plenty of good advice too, but Jess found the best teacher of all was Dodger. He just seemed to know exactly which cow she was after and wasted no time cutting it out. He pounced back and forth so quickly she sometimes had trouble staying in the saddle.

Her friends all took it in turns to practise their cut-outs, and then they set up a course of pegs in the big arena and galloped after the cattle. Stanley and Craig let each cow out of the arena after they'd had a run and chased them back down the laneway to the paddock.

By the end of the night, Jess was feeling charged. She and Dodger were drafting as well as any of her friends, if not better. As she washed him off and rugged him up for the night, she took a moment to scratch his cheeks and give him a cuddle. 'Shara was right about you. You're an absolute sweetie.' She ignored the pang in her gut that thoughts of Shara always brought, and focused on the campdraft. As she led Dodger out to his paddock, she felt her confidence rising. She had a chance of winning, she was sure. She thought of Wally and imagined how the little filly would look grazing next to Dodger in the paddocks at home.

20

'WHAT ABOUT this pair, Jessy?'

Jess poked her head out of the change room and saw Caroline holding up a pair of jeans, admiring them. 'Mum, they're *pink*.'

Caroline fingered the tag and turned it over, reading the label. 'Actually, they're watermelon. I used to have a pair of flares in exactly the same colour. Only in those days it was called flamingo.'

'They're for rodeos, Mum.'

'Isn't that what you're going to? I thought you were rounding up cows?'

'No, it's a campdraft! I'll look like a ninny in those,' Jess said, retreating behind the curtain.

Then Caroline called out, 'Oh, Jessy! Look at that *hat*!'

Jess looked out again. Her mother was staring at a mannequin wearing fringed chaps and a red ten-gallon hat with a band of silver sequins around the base and two yellow feathers jutting out the side. It was the most obscene thing Jess had ever laid eyes on. 'Thanks, but I already have my Akubra that you gave me for Christmas. It's perfect.'

Thank God.

'I was thinking more for myself,' said Caroline. She took the hat from the mannequin's head and walked to a long mirror near the change rooms. 'Oh, it's so fabulous! You know how some things jump out at you and you just have to have them?'

Jess came out of her change room in stiffly ironed dark blue jeans with a set of paper tags hanging from the belt loop. She bent her knees a couple of times and pulled at the waistband. 'These feel pretty good.'

Then she looked up and saw her mother, who was still admiring the red hat in the mirror. 'You are not wearing that to the campdraft, Mum. You'll frighten the cattle!'

'Oh, Jessy, don't be so dull,' said Caroline. She frowned at the jeans Jess was wearing and twirled her finger, indicating for Jess to turn on the spot. Jess obliged.

'Hmm, they're okay, I suppose,' Caroline said, clearly underwhelmed. Then she began sifting through another rack of jeans. 'How about these turquoise ones – they are much more interesting. This saddlery shop is fantastic. Why have we never been here before?'

'Mum, I told you, those ones are for rodeos. I just need

a pair of blue jeans. That's what Grace and Rosie wear.'

Caroline screwed up her nose. 'Okay, be boring. What about a shirt? Can we get you a nice shirt, or does that have to be boring as well?'

'What did you have in mind?' Jess asked cautiously.

'Oh, I don't know, just something nice.' Caroline pushed coathangers across the rack one at a time.

'Mum, don't you think you should take that hat off? The lady might think you want to buy it.'

'Oh, but I do, Jess. I absolutely love it and I need something to wear. I have to look smart too, you know!'

'Better than tie-dyed undies, I s'pose,' said Jess. 'Hang on – I like *this* one.'

Caroline pulled the shirt out from the rack. 'Ooh, that is nice. Well spotted, Jess.'

It was short-sleeved and made from soft, cool cotton. The front pockets were trimmed in bright pink piping and the yoke had pink and white stripes. Behind the shoulders were pleats to allow the wearer to move her arms while riding. It was quite funky, without being too much.

'I love it,' said Caroline. 'Try it on.'

Jess took the shirt back to the change room. It was absolutely perfect. She came out and paraded for her mother.

Caroline laid both hands over her heart. 'You look beautiful, darling.'

Jess slipped out of the shirt and jeans and tossed them over the change-room door to Caroline. She threw her old clothes on and gathered up the rejected outfits.

On her way to the counter Jess nearly ran into Shara, holding a bag with the shop's logo on it and making her way to the door. Jess's mouth gaped open and she nearly dropped the armful of clothes she was carrying.

Shara stared straight through her and strode past as though she couldn't get out of there fast enough. By the time Jess turned around, the shop door was swinging shut and as quickly as she had appeared, Shara was gone.

Jess looked to her mum. 'Did you see that?' she mouthed.

Caroline nodded from the front counter. Jess ran out into the street. She checked to the left and then along the row of shops to the right. She looked over the road and in the park, but there was no sign of Shara. It was as if she had imagined the whole thing. What a cow!

Jess stewed all the way home. 'I can't believe she just snobbed me off like that.'

'Yes, it was very strange, wasn't it?' agreed Caroline. 'She was very awkward with me at the counter, too.'

'What was she buying? Did you see?'

'No, she already had it in the bag.' Caroline shrugged.

'She didn't even say hello! She treated me like a total stranger!'

'Well, you two haven't spoken for months. She probably thought you would just snub her anyway.'

'I would not! No way would I snub Shara!'

Caroline raised her eyebrows but said nothing.

'What?' demanded Jess. 'I would not!'

'Well, that may not be the message you gave her down on the river flats that day,' said Caroline cautiously. 'Maybe she thinks you're still mad at her, which you are obviously—' she turned and searched her daughter's face for clues, '—not?'

'Of course I'm not!' said Jess angrily. 'Okay, not officially,' she amended. 'Well, what does she expect after first lying to me, then totally blocking me?'

'Didn't you block her first?'

'That's *different*. I had a reason to.'

'Why don't you give her a ring?' said Caroline. 'It's about time you two sorted things out, don't you think? Shara is like family to us.'

'No way, not after she just looked through me like that!' said Jess, crossing her arms tightly. She thought of the text messages they used to send. She didn't even carry her mobile around with her anymore. It had gone back to being what it was bought for – emergencies. 'I can't *believe* she didn't even say hello.'

'Oh, come on, Jess. She's your best friend,' said Caroline.

Jess stared out the window, fuming. 'Not anymore, she's not. I have new best friends.'

That afternoon, Jess sat under the trees in the mares' paddock watching Walkabout pick at fresh shoots of grass. In three months the little filly had nearly doubled in size, and her rump now stood higher than her shoulders as she grew one end at a time. Her foal fur had fallen out and she was a deep, glossy chestnut with a white snow-cap over her hindquarters. Even the fur around her neck had begun to grow back over the rope burns. It had taken weeks to earn her trust again after that incident. Jess had sat patiently each day under the tree, leaving a bread crust behind each time, until Walkabout felt safe enough to resume her old tricks.

Jess smiled as the filly walked towards her. 'Hi, beautiful girl,' she said, holding out a crust. 'We're heading off to the draft tonight. Everything's packed.'

She had been helping to load the truck ever since she got back from the shops. They had packed saddles, hay bales, swags and anything else they would possibly need. All that was left to load were the horses. Much to everyone's relief, Tegan and Katrina had given up the idea of campdrafting. Both girls had moved their horses elsewhere to resume their hacking and showing pursuits.

Walkabout took the crust and stood quietly munching at it, swishing her tail at the odd fly and stamping a back foot. Jess gave her a tickle under the chin. 'Thank God the poo-magnets aren't coming.'

The other kids would all travel to the draft in Harry's truck. It had a big double bunk and it was going to be a whole lot of fun. Craig and Caroline would follow in their ute. Lawson had reappeared since the scene with Ryan, but Grace had told Jess that he was making his own way there.

'I won't let him buy you, Wally,' she said, stroking the filly's neck. 'I'm going to win that draft and save you.'

The filly sniffed at Jess's face. Her muzzle was exquisitely soft and her breath sent goosebumps along Jess's arms.

Jess gave Walkabout a kiss on the cheek and looked into her gentle brown eyes. She could see her own reflection in them. 'I gotta go, little one.' She got up and walked out into the paddock while the filly trotted ahead. Two other foals pricked their ears, and then the three of them wheeled around and galloped off, bucking and squealing.

As she made her way back up the lane, she could hear the clatter of hooves on a tailgate up ahead and, as she got closer, the diesel engine of Harry's truck. Grace was dragging a reluctant Handbrake behind her up the ramp.

Luke stood at the top of the laneway. 'Come on, Jess!' he called out. 'Dodger goes on next!'

She broke into a run. This was it! It was happening. It was really happening!

Jess sat in the middle of the cabin seat, with Tom, Luke, Rosie and Grace squeezed in around her. A buzz of excitement ran between them as they organised pillows for the long journey. Ahead, Stanley Arnold led the convoy, towing a huge red gooseneck trailer. Caroline and Craig followed behind.

The two-way radio made a fuzzy noise and Stanley's voice crackled into life through the cabin. 'You get off all right, Harry?'

Harry took a mouthpiece from the centre console and replied, 'Longwood, here we come!'

Grace stuck her head out the window and let the wind catch her hair. 'So long, Porpoise Spit!' she yelled.

Rosie and Jess leaned over and stuck their heads out with her, and they all yelled, 'So long, Coachwood Crossing!'

'Er, Harry.' This time Craig's voice crackled on the

two-way. 'Can you tell those kids to get themselves back inside the truck?'

Harry grabbed the mouthpiece again. 'Will do, Craig.' He double-shuffled the truck up a gear and said, 'Come on, you lot. Get your ugly mugs back inside the cabin. And put some seatbelts on.'

Grace ripped open a large bag of jersey caramels. 'What have you got?' she asked, diving uninvited into Jess's backpack and pulling out the healthy wholemeal muffins lovingly baked by Caroline, which Jess had absolutely no intention of eating. She had slipped a few to Dodger earlier and he thought they were delicious. And strangely, so did Grace. After one bite, she eagerly swapped her entire stash of caramels for them. 'You are *so* lucky to get home baking,' she said, as she munched. 'Kwor, these are yummo!'

'Go for it,' said Jess, unwrapping a caramel. She saw Luke eyeing off the muffins. 'Help yourself,' she said, surprised that they were so popular.

Soon the floor of the cabin was littered with little silver papers and food wrappers.

Within a couple of hours, the sun peeled back over the mountain range and dusk descended. They drove through the darkness, stopping only briefly to refuel and grab a burger at a highway truckstop. As they travelled further west, the night grew colder and colder.

Jess sat in the cabin of the truck looking out the window, marvelling at how brightly the moon lit the wide, grassy downs on either side of the road. She could make out the silhouettes of grazing cattle, and at one stage a rabbit bounded across in front of them.

Hours later, a line of telegraph poles guided them into the sleeping town of Longwood.

Hundreds of horse trucks were already parked at the showgrounds, and webs of white tape, set up to yard sleeping horses, wove in and out between them. They found Stanley, who had saved a spot for them, unloaded the weary horses and bedded them down for what was left of the night.

With the horses out, Harry's truck converted into a comfortable camper. The top end had a small kitchenette with a gas stove and fridge and a fluorescent light running off batteries. Wire racks ran the length of the truck above head height, housing saddlery, blankets and luggage. While Harry and the boys bunked in the cabin of the truck, the girls swept out the back, unrolled their swags and, after much whispering and giggling, put their heads down to sleep.

Jess lay there listening to the distant sounds of trucks on the highway and cattle crooning. Muffled country music crackled out of a radio and someone clunked about in the back of a horse float. She could hear men laughing a short distance away. On the other side of the truck's metal walls, Dodger ripped noisily at his haynet and snorted dust from his nostrils.

Finally she was in Longwood. This was her destiny. She could feel it!

21

RATTLING FEED BINS and bellowing cattle woke Jess. She hauled herself out of her swag, climbed over her slumbering friends and peeked out of the narrow door of the truck.

Before her, the harsh country was softened by the gentle morning sun and a morning dew. Silver leaves shimmered on the boree trees that were dotted about. The day stretched out before her, as yet untouched, promising things new and exciting. Jess grabbed her jacket and crept out the door.

On the other side of the truck, the arena was already filled with riders. Stockmen moved bellowing cattle from yard to yard, smacking their rumps with hollow pipes. Road trains lined up at the gates, waiting to unload more dusty, dung-covered cattle, while local townsfolk arrived in rusty utes to see the big event. The smell of frying bacon and eggs from the breakfast tent wafted tantalisingly through the air.

'Hey, Dodger,' Jess said. She stroked his glossy neck, thinking about the huge task they both had in front of them. 'You're a good boy. Even if we don't win, you're still a good boy.'

The horse waggled his ears and Jess took a moment to give them a scratch, before doling out morning feeds and topping up water buckets.

A crackly voice on the loudspeaker split the early-morning quiet. 'Good morning, competitors, and welcome to the Twenty-Fifth Annual Longwood Campdraft! Our first event for the day is the maiden draft, which is sponsored by Mac Feeds and will begin in fifteen minutes. We have over twelve hundred cattle to put through the yards this weekend, so, people, please be ready when your name is called.'

Grace's voice came out of nowhere. 'I went to the secretary's tent and got your number in the draw, Jessy.'

Jess turned and saw her sitting on the tailgate of the truck in flannelette pyjama bottoms and an old T-shirt, sipping a cup of tea. 'You're number ninety-two,' Grace said. 'You're lucky – you won't be on for ages.'

Rosie stumbled out into the daylight in pyjamas that matched her sister's. 'Grace and I are both on early,' she moaned. 'I'm twenty-four and Grace is seventeen.' She plonked herself heavily on her bottom and stared into space. 'I hate mornings.'

'Dad got us some brekkie,' said Grace, nodding towards a small camping table. On it sat three bundles of paper towel with greasy patches seeping through.

Jessica's mouth watered. 'Is that third one for me?' she asked hopefully.

'Uh huh,' nodded Grace, reaching over and passing her a bundle.

Jess bit into an egg-and-bacon sandwich. The crispy bacon tasted extra delicious in fluffy white bread. 'This is so yummy,' she mumbled. 'Sure beats wheatgrass juice and buckwheat muffins!'

'You're in cattle country now,' said Rosie. 'Wait till you taste the steak sambos.'

'Yeah, Dad reckons you can tell a good draft by their steak sambos,' said Grace. 'They stake their reputations on it!' She nudged Jess. 'Get it? Steak . . . their reputations? Get it? They're cattle farmers?'

Jess groaned.

'Hey, the poo-magnet's here,' said Rosie, as she bit into her sandwich. 'I saw her over near the hacking ring. That horse of hers nearly blinded me.'

'Thank God she's not drafting,' said Jess.

'She'll find some way to cause trouble,' said Rosie, yawning and stretching. 'Harry reckons we should go into the arena and help the stewards put cattle away. That way we can practise a bit. I'm going to go and get some jeans on.'

'Okay,' said Jess.

She saddled Dodger as he finished his grain and then let him digest his breakfast while she changed into her riding clothes. She spent a few minutes in the back of the truck, plaiting her hair and polishing her boots, and as she did so she imagined herself riding a perfect round.

I have to get a good beast.

She buckled up her helmet as she walked out the door. She was ready.

Dodger nickered and stamped his foot.

'Righto, boy, let's do this,' she said, pulling his bridle over his ears. She walked him over to the practice arena.

Dodger felt good. Seasoned horse that he was, he was fit and energetic without being over-excited. Handbrake, meanwhile, trotted lazily behind them.

'Wanna swap horses?' Grace said to Jess as she urged the young mare to catch up. 'I'm up next and I can barely stop her from snoring.'

'No, thanks!' Jess laughed.

The girls reached the camp-yard gate and Jess wished Grace good luck. She stayed and watched Grace kick hopelessly at Handbrake's sides while her chosen beast darted back to the mob. In less than a minute, the judge, who sat outside the camp on his horse, lifted his arm, gave a sharp crack of his whip and disqualified her. Jess gave her a pat on the back as she came back out of the camp.

'Old donkey,' said Grace. 'How come I always get stuck with the crap horses?'

'Because you can never just stick to one horse,' said Rosie.

'Because you're the most adventurous rider,' said Jess. 'You're good at training them.'

'Wish Dad would find a buyer for her so I can start training something decent,' said Grace as she led the mare back to the truck.

The announcer called another series of numbers.

'My turn!' said Rosie, in alarm. She rode Buster into the camp. After a great cut-out, she burst through the gates and shouldered a small heifer around the first two pegs before it frolicked off to the sidelines and went off course.

Jess clapped madly, and then took Dodger for a walk around the grounds. She visualised her perfect round over and over in her head, imagined galloping after the beast and shouldering it around the pegs. She went over everything she had learned.

Keep your legs forward, supple waist, soft hands, pick a good beast, stay off its heels.

By the time the announcer called her name, Jess could

no longer think. She could no longer plan or practise. She just had to go out there and do it. All that remained between now and Walkabout's destiny were five other kids, lined up outside the camp, and about thirteen and a half minutes. She took a deep breath.

The camp yard was made from steel railings and screened with hessian so the cattle couldn't see out. Jess sat on Dodger, looking over the top rail. At one end a small mob of mixed-breed cattle huddled together. At the other a stockman stood behind a large set of gates, ready to let the next rider and his chosen beast out into the main arena. A judge sat near the gates on a grey horse, holding a stockwhip in one hand, reins in the other. A scorer sat on the fence nearby, with a small chalkboard.

Jess took her place in line with several other competitors outside the yard as a boy entered through a narrow side gate. He nodded to the judge, picked a beast and began trying to cut it from the herd. His pony darted back and forth while the rider kicked madly. The beast scooted away, and in his excitement, the boy and his horse charged straight into the mob, scattering them about the pen. Jess frowned as she watched him chase them into a frenzy.

'Oh, good on ya,' said a girl in a loud voice. She pointed at the cattle that were now crushing up against the back fence, trying to climb out. 'Now they're all panicked. He's wrecking it for everyone. They shouldn't let beginners ride at championship events.'

Jess tried to tune out.

I thought they used quiet old dairy cattle for the juniors.

When the boy had clearly lost control of his beast, the judge's whip split the air, disqualifying him. The stockman opened the gates to let him out and three steers escaped after him.

'At least that got rid of a few jumpy ones,' said the girl next to her. 'Glad you're on next and not me.'

Jess forced a smile which she hoped exuded confidence and experience. On the microphone she heard the announcer introducing herself and Dodger.

'Ladies and gentlemen, this next horse has seen a cattleyard or two. He's by a local stallion called Rough Nut, and I guarantee he'll give any beast a run for its money. Originally owned and bred by the Hayward family on Triple Bar Stud, he's been carting juniors around the drafts for nigh on twenty years. He's a pocket dynamo, this one, ladies and gentlemen. Let's see what he can do today!'

Jess listened in astonishment. The announcer knew more about Dodger than she did.

A stockman ushered her inside the small pen, where a dozen or so rangy beasts stared at her with goggle eyes. People were perched along the rails in boots and broad-brimmed hats, watching her.

In the distance, a judge sashed a brilliant white horse with a blue ribbon.

Don't even think about her.

In the stands, a red hat stood out amid rows of brown Akubras. Both Caroline and Craig were waving madly.

Stay focused. Find a good beast, just peel it off the edge of the mob and call for the gate.

A tall Aboriginal stockman in a big black hat walked up to her. 'Bin a while since them cattle have been handled,' he said. 'You wanna give them some time to settle.'

Jess nodded. She couldn't agree more. The cattle were agitated and twitchy, and bellowed whenever she moved. Too soon, the judged called for her to start. She had ten seconds to begin.

A deep red steer with big shoulders broke away from the mob, rushing down the side fence. It wasn't the kind of animal she was looking for, but she took her chance, slipping Dodger in behind it and placing herself between it and the mob.

This is for you, Wally.

The steer darted to the end of the yard and, finding itself alone, did an about-face and bolted back towards the others. Dodger shot out from under Jess and galloped into its path. The beast slid to a stop. It broke away to the right. Jess grabbed the front of her saddle as Dodger spun away again. He galloped three strides to the fence and slammed to a halt with a jolt that made her wince, but she managed to rein him back to the centre of the yard.

Jess held the saddle tight and sat deep. She could barely keep up with Dodger's rushes from side to side. Fortunately, neither could the beast. It gave up, ran to the front of the yard and slammed up against the gates, bellowing loudly and swishing its tail. From somewhere, she could hear whistles and a dull roar.

'Gate!' she yelled to the gate men. They swung them open, and the beast whooshed out of the yard into the main arena as though it were being sucked into a black hole. Dodger leapt after it. His hooves thundered over the freshly ploughed ground. He flew up behind on the tail of the beast. Jess brought him up onto the steer's shoulder at a full gallop. Dodger leaned heavily and pushed it around the first peg in a wide loop.

She wrestled Dodger back behind the beast for the crossover.

Without warning, the steer stopped abruptly and she and Dodger went flying by. Dodger hit the skids. He ducked back to the beast and took control again. It headed towards the second peg at a slightly slower pace, and Dodger settled comfortably on its shoulder, bringing it around in an easy loop. They headed for the final gate.

This is it; we're going to make it . . .

Abruptly, the rhythm in Dodger's stride broke. He paddled wildly as he tried to regain balance. Jess lurched out of the saddle. She wrapped her arms around his neck, and closed her eyes tight, waiting for the earth to swallow them up. She felt a bump and Dodger skidded to a stop, grinding a long smooth channel into the ploughed earth.

She looked down and saw a mangled horseshoe hanging from the side of Dodger's hoof. As two stockmen galloped out to her, she slipped off his neck and onto the ground.

'I'm fine,' she said to the men, and bent down to pick up Dodger's foot. A large piece of hoof had been ripped away with the shoe. One of the stockmen jumped off his horse and helped to remove it, pulling carefully so as not to cause any further damage.

'Better get a farrier onto that foot, love,' he said, shaking his head. 'It'll take some artwork to get a shoe back on that.' Then he pointed at the finish flag next to her. 'By geez, you just made that by the skin of your teeth.'

'Did I finish?' asked Jess, unsure if she had blown it or not.

'Judge called an eighty-two,' he said, giving her a nod of approval. 'That oughta put you in the finals tomorrow.

That's if you can get that hoof fixed. Lawson Blake is on the ground. If anyone can fix that mess, it's him. He could put shoes on a mosquito.'

Lawson Blake? He's not touching my horse!

Jess led Dodger from the arena, relieved to find he was not lame. His hoof, however, was a mess. There was no way she could ride him in the second round without a new shoe.

At the truck, she pulled her saddle off and rubbed Dodger down with an old towel.

Harry limped over to congratulate her. 'Great round, Jess. Well done. Eighty-two is a darn good score for your first go.'

But Jess was far from happy. She held up the mangled shoe. 'Look at his foot, Harry. It's a mess.'

'Is that what happened?' Harry raised an eyebrow. 'I saw him have a bit of a stumble at the end of the round. I thought he just lost his footing.'

'He ripped off the shoe with his back foot. He must have overreached.'

Harry ran a hand down Dodger's leg and picked up his foot. He let out a breezy whistle. 'You've done a job on that, haven't ya, fella!' He dropped the foot and gave the horse a slap on the neck. 'You wanna get Lawson to look at that. He could put shoes on a mosquito.'

Some sort of local saying?

Jess felt her heart run down into her boots. 'I know he's your son, Harry, but I really don't want to ask him.'

'You'll find he's not such a bad bloke, Jess. He's your only hope at this stage.'

Jess sighed and gave Dodger a pat. He was frothy with sweat and needed a good hose down and a drink. So did she. The day was growing hotter and a westerly wind had come up. Dust blew through the air, drying Jess's throat and scratching at her eyes. She led Dodger to the horse wash and filled a bucket. The water was deliciously cool and she was tempted to stick her whole head into it.

Suddenly she felt a sharp push on the back of her legs and her knees buckled. She spun around. A familiar slobbering dog grinned at her.

'Hex!' said Jess in astonishment. 'What are you doing here?' There was no mistaking that blue eye and the chunk missing from the tip of his ear. Hex jumped up, leaving two muddy streaks on the front of her jeans. 'Get down!' she growled, pushing him off.

At that moment, Katrina Pettilow walked past leading Chelpie. The pony was immaculate, her hooves painted glossy black and mane plaited into neat little baubles, and her neck was covered with blue ribbons. Katrina smiled. 'Now who's the poo-magnet?'

A sharp whistle made Jess turn. 'Shara!'

'Hex, come here,' said Shara, ignoring Jess. At her feet sat Petunia, panting in the heat. Behind them both, tied to the side of the float, was Rocko, swishing his tail at a fly and picking at a net of hay. It was like déjà vu. Jess had spent so many weekends with Diamond tied to the other side of that horse float: Rocko on the right and Diamond on the left. Her first instinct was to throw her arms around Shara and jump up and down in excitement.

But Shara's face was hard and closed. She whistled up her dogs and walked back behind the float. Jess turned to the tap and made herself busy, filling a bucket with cool, clean water for Dodger, while her mind whirled with hurt and disbelief.

What was Shara doing here?

22

THE LOUDSPEAKER BOOMED. 'This is the final competitor in the first round of the juniors, ladies and gentlemen, and it's Shara Wilson on Rocko. He looks like a handy little fella, and young Shara seems to have a good handle on him. Some very nice blocking manoeuvres from the horse.'

Jess listened to the announcer's seamless monologue from the back of the truck. She couldn't believe Shara was here in the middle of the outback. It didn't seem possible.

'Nice control of the beast around the first peg, and just look at that horse go, ladies and gentlemen, and she nearly lost it at the finish pegs, but she seems to be back on its heels, a very gutsy performance out there. And her time is up but a very tidy round, and the judge has given her a score of eighty-two, which will put her in the finals tomorrow.'

It was the same score as Jess's. Shara had always talked

about campdrafting. But here? Now? In Longwood?

The next event was the open draft. Jess wanted to see Harry ride Biyanga. He had been so disappointed about his two sons fighting that he'd decided to ride the stallion himself. He reckoned he was too old and creaky to get around the whole course, but he was going to try to win the highest cut-out score. The top ten scores would be eligible for a competition the next day and Harry had his sights set on that trophy.

Leaving Dodger to eat his lunch, Jess made her way to the grandstand. She was relieved to find Tom and Luke sitting way up the back where there was no chance of running into Shara.

'Hey, great round,' said Tom, as she joined them.

'What happened at the end?' asked Luke. 'Dodger stumble?'

'He overreached,' said Jess. 'He's pulled a shoe and torn up his foot.'

'Lawson could—' Luke stopped mid-sentence.

'Yeah, don't tell me, he could put shoes on a mosquito,' said Jess glumly. 'Not likely he'll help me, though.'

'Maybe there's another farrier on the grounds,' he suggested.

'Apparently not,' said Jess.

'Hey, here comes that girl again,' said Tom suddenly.

'Which girl?' asked Jess, looking across the grounds.

She saw Shara, riding past the grandstand on Rocko.

'Shara Wilson,' said Tom. 'I've seen her at a few drafts lately.'

'A few drafts?' said Jess. 'I can't believe it. She never told me she was drafting!'

Tom and Luke stared at her. 'How do you know her?' asked Tom.

'Who are you talking about?' Grace shuffled across to join them.

'Shara Wilson,' said Tom.

'She's Jess's best friend,' said Grace. 'Well, she used to be.'

'We don't talk much anymore,' said Jess.

'She's a red-hot rider,' said Tom.

'Who's a red-hot rider?' asked Rosie, appearing from behind them.

'Shara Wilson.' Tom turned to Luke. 'Brilliant horse. What's the name of her horse?'

Jess noticed Rosie scowl.

'Rocky, I think,' said Luke.

'It's Rocko,' said Jess flatly.

She saw Lawson outside the camp and took the opportunity to change the subject. 'Hey, look. There's Lawson. The novice event must have started.'

Lawson rode into the camp on a big chestnut mare and nodded to the judge. He wore jeans and a rusty red shirt, and on his boots were long-shanked spurs. He faced the cattle and danced the mare back and forth to warm her up. A bundle of nerves and jitters, she dived madly into the mob, surfacing with a lanky black steer.

The mare put in several good blocks, only to have the beast duck back to the mob. Lawson faced her up again and brought the steer to the front of the camp. He called for the gate and let the steer race out, completing the course and scoring a seventy-eight.

'He still did a good job on that beast,' said Luke.

'Yeah,' said Grace. 'Even though he had two goes at cutting it.'

'I think that's his good mare, Marnie,' said Tom. 'She's only young. He probably just wants to give her a bit of experience. Not much point in pushing her too hard in the camp.'

'Since when does *he* care about that sort of thing?' grumbled Jess.

Harry was next. Biyanga looked magnificent in a fancy bridle with shiny buckles. With a nod to the judge, Harry squeezed him forward and began his cut-out. Biyanga walked calmly to the mob and singled out a black heifer. He followed it to the front of the yard and ducked quickly to block it as it dashed back and forth. Harry and the stallion danced easily from left to right, pushing the beast steadily to the front of the camp, and when it was clear that the bleating young heifer was under his complete control, Harry called for the gate. As it shot into the arena, the old man brought Biyanga to a sliding halt and let it go.

'And *that*, ladies and gentlemen, is how you cut a beast!' said the announcer excitedly. 'That's a twenty-four cut-out, folks. You won't see a better score than that this weekend! We'll see Harry Blake and Biyanga in the cut-out competition tomorrow, and what an event it will be with that calibre of horsemanship.'

Tom and Luke jumped to their feet, clapping and whistling with the rest of the audience. Jess stood up and clapped too, but although she was happy for Harry, she couldn't get her mind off Shara and Rocko.

Had Shara known Jess was going to be here? Was she purposely trying to freak her out? Was she trying to stop her from winning the draft? Why would she do that to her? She was so cold.

As the others raced down the stands and back to the truck to see Harry, Jess walked off in the other direction. It was time to get some answers, not just second-hand whispers and gossip. Why would her best friend, her longest and truest friend, and someone she shared everything with, hide the truth from her?

She was determined to find out.

Jess walked into the stable block and found Rocko's unmistakably chunky head hanging over a stable door. Shara was inside, picking out his feet.

Jess stood at the door. 'Tell me what happened, Shara. How did Diamond get out of her paddock?'

Shara threw a hoofpick into a bucket and grabbed a brush. 'Oh, hello to you too. Yes, I've been well, thank you. How about you?' She brushed Rocko with short, sharp strokes, keeping her back to Jess.

'How did she end up in that cattle grid, Shara?'

'How would I know?'

'You must have been there. You saw it happen, didn't you?'

Shara spun around and glared at her. 'I did *not* see it happen. Do you really think I would just walk away and leave Diamond lying in a cattle grid? Who told you that?'

'Why won't you tell me about it, then?'

Shara kept brushing Rocko and said nothing.

'Shara!'

'What? I told you, I didn't see it happen. Now go away and leave me alone.'

Jess didn't move.

Silence.

Rocko screwed up his nose and took a swipe at the horse in the next stable. Shara stopped brushing. 'I swear I don't know, Jess.'

'Then just tell me what you do know,' said Jess, her voice softening, pleading. All this mystery was tearing her apart. 'Why are you being so horrible to me? What have I done?'

Shara let out a deep sigh. 'Okay.' She put an arm over Rocko's back. 'When I went down to the river flats that morning, the horses were out and Rocko was chasing Diamond around. I tried to catch him, but he charged at me and bit me.' She rolled up her sleeve and showed Jess a red crescent-shaped scar on her upper arm. 'Rocko was really upset about something. I've never seen him like that.'

'Why didn't you get me to come and help you?'

'I couldn't. I was supposed to be cleaning out the shed and Mum had told me not to go down there until I'd finished my jobs.'

'But that's a really bad bite. Surely you needed a doctor, surely that was more important than a few jobs? Your folks would be more worried about your arm.'

'Mum hated Rocko enough already, everybody did, they still do. If she knew about this bite, there's no way she'd let me keep him. He would have been sent straight back to the doggers. I couldn't tell her.'

Jess stood there, confused. Rocko screwed up his nose and shook his head at her.

Shara continued. 'I thought the horses would be okay

while I went back and finished the shed. I was going to go back down and catch them in the afternoon, and then I got that letter from Canningdale. When I went around to your place to tell you, I was also going to get you to help me round them up. But I was too late.'

'So, does your mum know now? That Rocko bit you?' asked Jess.

Shara tightened her mouth and said nothing.

'She doesn't know,' said Jess. 'How could you keep that scar hidden?'

'I told her it was a different horse, some other horse down there. I wasn't sure which one, because it all happened so fast.' She gave Jess a *don't-you-dare-tell-her-otherwise* look.

'So when did Diamond get stuck in the grid?' asked Jess.

'I don't know – sometime between when I saw her and when you found her, I guess. I swear I didn't know she was hurt, Jess. There is no way I would have left her.'

'So how did the horses get out?'

Shara held her hands up. 'I don't know. Rocko has never gone through a fence before.'

'Neither had Diamond.'

They both stared at each other.

'Why didn't you tell me, Shara? I was your best friend. We told each other everything. Soul sisters, remember?'

This was the bit that confounded Jess. 'Didn't you trust me?'

'Jess, your horse had a broken leg. You were distraught. If you thought it was Rocko, if you'd seen my arm, you would have said Rocko was vicious too.'

He is!

Shara saw the look on Jess's face. 'See. I knew you'd think so! Everyone thinks he's dangerous. Dad would have made me get rid of him, and there's no way I could find a good home for a horse like him. He would have had to die too. I just couldn't do it.' Shara was beginning to sound upset.

Jess stared at Shara's scar. 'I never thought he'd do *that.*'

Shara rolled her sleeve further down. 'I was going to tell you when we went for that ride, but Katrina showed up, then Lawson, then you were too busy having a hissy fit!'

'My face was smashed in!' said Jess, beginning to get angry again.

'I know it was,' said Shara. 'So what was I supposed to do? I stuffed up! I'm sorry!'

'You blocked my phone number.'

'You blocked me first.'

Jess scowled.

'Were there any cattle down on the flats?' she asked.

'Maybe they pushed the fence down.'

'None of ours were, just Lawson Blake's,' said Shara. 'They were way up the other end, nowhere near her. But they were really stirred up. Whatever spooked Diamond through that fence must have spooked those cattle too.'

'I bet it was Lawson letting off a gunshot!' said Jess.

'Yeah, I wondered about that, but I would have heard it.'

'Maybe he did it the day before? Maybe they were out all night.'

'No, I was down there the day before. The fence was fine. They were still in their own paddocks.'

Jess sighed. It looked as though she would never know what happened.

'I'm so sorry you lost Diamond, Jessy. I think about her all the time. I really miss her too.'

Jess nodded.

'Is that a new horse you're riding?'

'That's Dodger.'

'Dodger?' Shara squeaked.

'Changed, hasn't he?' Jess grinned.

'Sure has,' said Shara, sounding bewildered.

'I found a little filly called Walkabout. I want to buy her. She's an Appaloosa.'

'Like Diamond.'

'Do you believe in reincarnation, Shara?'

'In what?' asked Shara, slipping a bridle over Rocko's head and buckling it up. 'Oh shivers, I better go, I'm on in a minute.' She reached for her saddle.

'Reincarnation — you know, when you come back as something else after you die.'

'Dunno, never really thought about it,' Shara said, pulling up the girth straps. She walked around to the stable door, and brought Rocko after her.

Jess told Shara about Walkabout, being born on the same day Diamond had died. 'It's weird, I know, but she is just so much like Diamond. She follows me all around the paddock as though she knows me.'

Shara put her foot up to a stirrup.

'Lawson Blake wants to buy her.' Jess continued. 'You know how horrible he is. I just can't bear the thought of Wally being in his hands. She'll be abused—'

'Sorry, Jess. I've gotta fly,' said Shara. 'I'm in the Novice!'

As Jess watched Shara disappear behind a truck, she heard a throat clear behind her. She spun around.

Lawson was leaning against the stable wall on the other side of the aisle. He must have heard the whole conversation. He gave her a cold look and then strode out of the building.

23

'ARE YOU COMING over to the bonfire, Jess?' asked Grace. 'Harry's playing the banjo and Lawson's brought his guitar. It'll be great!'

'Nah, I'm going to get an early night,' said Jess, pretending to clean her saddle. She had spent the afternoon in the back of Harry's truck, avoiding everyone.

'Oh come on, Jess. We've got marshmallows!' Grace sang, waving a bag. 'Yummy, yummy, hot and gooey!'

'I don't feel like it, Grace. I'm just going to go to bed.' Jess folded her polishing cloth and tossed it into her grooming bag.

'Cum*maahn*! Rosie is all smoochied up with Tom, it's gross, and I've got no one to hang out with. Please?'

Jess wished Grace would go away. She just wanted to crawl into her sleeping bag and sort out her head. 'I'm really tired, Grace.'

'Are you still upset about Dodger's foot?'

'Yeah, a little bit.'

'Oh, okay then. You're dismissed,' groaned Grace. 'Have a good sleep.' She ran off to join the others around the fire.

As Jess crawled into her swag, she could hear Harry's wheezy voice singing over the crackle of the fire. She mulled over everything that had happened so far, and realised that the only way she could win the draft now was to get Dodger's foot fixed. The only person who could do that, it seemed, was Lawson Blake – and she was not about to ask him for a favour.

The weekend hadn't gone to plan at all. She had blown any hope of winning the draft, or saving Walkabout. She rolled over in her swag and her spine hit a bump on the truck floor. She thought of her soft, warm bed at home and wondered what she was even doing there.

'Jessy! Wake up!' Grace shook her violently. 'Wake up, Jess! The horses are out!'

'What?' Jess rolled over, rubbing her eyes.

'Katrina tied Chelpie to the fence near Muscles, and he went crazy. He smashed through his yard and tore through electric fences.'

'He did what?' Jess crawled out of her swag and squinted into the torch that Grace shone in her face.

'And then Dodger and three of Lawson's horses escaped onto the road! '

'Oh, my God! Which way did they go?' asked Jess, scrambling to the door.

'They went out the front gate. Dad and Harry have headed towards town and we have to go the other way to see if we can find them.' Grace motioned to Jess with one arm. 'Come on. Quick!'

'Muscles is a stallion. He'll attack Dodger,' said Jess, wrapping her arms tightly around herself as she hurried through the freezing showgrounds. 'He'll hurt him.'

'No, he won't. He's not aggressive,' said Grace.

'Lawson's horses are all mares. Muscles will fight Dodger for them,' said Jess. 'He might get hit by a car . . . or get chased through a fence.' The more she woke up, the more she started freaking. 'We have to find them!' She broke into a run. 'Oh God, please don't let Dodger get hurt!'

The girls dashed through the maze of horse trucks and floats. They could see where the horses had torn through the electric tapes, leaving a tangled white trail behind. At the front entrance, Jess panted, already out of breath. 'Which way did they go?'

'That way is into town, so we have to go this way,' said Grace, taking off in the other direction. 'This torch is dying.'

'It doesn't matter. The moon is so bright it makes no difference anyway.' Jess ran alongside her. The road was coarse beneath her feet, and before long her socks had eroded away and were flapping around her ankles, leaving her feet rasping cruelly against the cold bitumen. She slowed to a hobble. 'This is hopeless. We will never catch up with five horses.'

Then she heard them. 'I can hear hooves on the road, listen! They're up ahead! They sound as though they're galloping.'

Then there came the most sickening sound. An air horn honked long and loud in the distance, accompanied by the screeching of brakes. 'Oh *no!*' Jess screamed and took off, leaving Grace behind her. Her feet stung with every step.

In front of them stretched miles of nothingness, with a corrugated dirt road through the middle of it. A road train rumbled in the distance, getting louder and louder until its lights rose up over a small rise in the land and came hurtling through the stillness of the outback towards her.

Jess dived into the grassy edges of the road as wheel after wheel thundered past. She counted four large bogies after the prime mover. Clouds of dust infused with cowdung billowed up behind it. She pulled her pyjama top over her mouth to filter the air, and closed her eyes tight. She couldn't see a thing.

Then, as she groped around blindly in the long grass, she trod on some overgrown mutant bindii burr. As she tried to extract it from her frozen foot, she wondered where Grace was.

A vehicle rumbled along the dirt road in her direction. Its headlights shone weakly through the blur of dust, its engine slowed and a gruff voice said, 'Get in, idiot!'

'Lawson?'

'Well, don't just sit there. Do you want a ride or not?'

Grace shifted across the bench seat to let her in. 'It's okay, Jess, hop in,' she said.

Luke stood on the back of the ute, holding onto the rollbar with one hand and working a large spotlight with the other. Lawson's blue pup raced around his feet.

Jess scrambled into the cabin. Unable to find a spot for her feet among the tools and debris on the passenger side floor, she pulled her knees up and sat cross-legged with her feet under her bum. She shivered with cold.

'I don't know what you kids thought you were going to do when you found those horses.' Lawson began a lecture. 'You're in the middle of the outback, with no shoes on, in the middle of the night! You've got no halters and one of those horses is a stallion with a mob of mares. Are you trying to get yourself killed?'

Pig.

Jess sat there in silence. The corrugations in the road

made the ute pound like a jackhammer, and it felt as though her brain was being rattled out of her skull. Lawson sped furiously along the track while she held white-knuckled onto the dash, bracing herself against the potholes as the ute lurched and bumped and fishtailed madly. Eventually he slowed down and peered intently out the window, as Luke shone the spotlight back and forth across the empty plains.

Lawson pulled his head back in and spoke as he drove. 'It wasn't me, you know.'

'What wasn't?' said Jess. Her hand flew against the side window for balance as they met a large pothole.

'It wasn't me who put that horse through the fence.'

'Hey?' She could hardly hear him above the chains and tools that rattled and clanked about. What was he talking about?

'You owned that little coloured horse, didn't you, the one that got stuck in the cattle grid?'

Jess's hackles rose. 'Diamond was an Appaloosa. What about her?'

'That white horse has been stirring up my cattle for weeks. I keep finding it loose down on the river. I tried to tell you at the old man's place that day, but you wouldn't listen.' He kept driving for a while. 'I thought it was you and your mad mate. But then I started finding Snow-bloody-white down there.'

He fought the steering wheel through another pothole. 'I'd be willing to bet that's how your pony got out and into that cattle grid. That white thing's the nastiest little horse I've ever handled. The other horses hate it. So do the cattle. Look at the trouble it's caused tonight.'

Luke thumped on the back window of the cabin. 'There they are!' They saw several shadowy horses beside the road.

'Oh, *great!*' said Lawson, as he wrenched on the hand-brake. In the headlights, Muscles grunted up and down on his best mare, Marnie. 'Get off her, you mongrel!' He got out, pulled a stockwhip from the back of the ute and cracked it at the stallion. The sound echoed into the distant hills.

Muscles leapt off, screaming defiance, and immediately began hunting Chelpie and the other two mares. Lawson continued to crack the whip at him and managed to get himself in between the stallion and the mares. Muscles pawed at the ground with one hoof and bared his teeth.

'Luke, grab Marnie, quick,' Lawson yelled. 'Grace, you get Muscles. Hurry up!'

'No *way*!' said Grace, standing by the ute, terrified.

'He'll be right as soon as you get your hand on his halter, Gracie. Just grab him!'

'He'll savage me,' pleaded Grace.

Muscles paced back and forth snorting and pawing at the ground as Lawson held him off with the whip, while Luke approached the mare and slipped a halter over her ears.

'If you don't grab him soon he's going to savage *me*,' he yelled at Grace, as Muscles rushed him with bared teeth. 'Come on, he's your horse.'

'He's not mine, he's Dad's,' she argued. At that moment, Dodger came into view. Muscles reared into the air and screamed, warning the gelding to keep away.

'Dodger! Get out of there!' yelled Jess.

'For Pete's sake, someone just get a rope and *grab him*!' Lawson yelled.

Jess grabbed a lead rope from the front of the ute and began to walk towards Muscles, who was transfixed on the three mares behind Lawson. She walked gingerly, trying to avoid the stones and burrs. 'Easy, Muscles,' she said.

The stallion turned and rushed at her with his ears back. Jess stopped immediately, ready to take flight if he got too close. She repeated the words, 'Easy, Muscles. Come here, boy,' and inched towards him, her hand trembling. She stayed focused on the ring at the bottom of his halter. The stallion let out a long, squealing whinny to the mares.

'That's it; good, Jess,' said Lawson. 'Just get that rope on him and he'll settle right down . . . slowly . . .'

Jess crept closer, keeping her bare feet as far out of reach of the stallion's steel-clad hooves as she could, and holding the rope out in front of her. Then she lurched forward and snapped the clip onto his halter. The moment it was attached, Lawson dropped his whip and ran to take the lead rope and pull the stallion into line. Jess stumbled backwards to get out of the way and fell over, finding another mutant burr with her hand.

'Come on, you old rogue,' said Lawson. 'The game's up.' He gave a tug on the stallion's halter. 'By geez, Stan's going to hear about this one.' He led the stallion back to the ute, who pranced and squealed cheekily. Then he turned to Jess. 'Well done, kid.'

Jess was unable to speak. Her hands were shaking.

'Wow! You were amazing, Jess!' called Grace, leading Dodger towards them. 'Weren't you scared?'

'I was totally petrified!' Jess tried not to burst into tears.

'Just wait a minute, Grace,' interrupted Lawson. 'Let me tie this stallion to a tree before you bring that gelding over.' He led Muscles to a scrawny mulga sapling and tied him securely.

'Is he okay?' asked Jess, hobbling towards Dodger. She threw her arms around his neck. She couldn't bear it if anything had happened to him. Suddenly the draft didn't matter; she just wanted Dodger to be okay.

'He seems to be. I can't really see. We need a torch,' said Grace.

'Bring him in front of the headlights,' said Lawson.

Jess took the lead rope from Grace and brought Dodger in front of the lights. 'I think he just has a few scratches.' Then she picked up his hoof and groaned. Another big chunk had been torn off.

'Give me a look,' said Lawson, returning from tethering Muscles. He placed the hoof between his knees and examined it carefully under the headlights. 'What a disaster,' he said. He dropped the hoof to the ground. 'So, how are we going to get all these horses back to the showgrounds?'

'Well, is it fixable or not?' asked Jess.

'We can't leave that stallion out here,' he said, ignoring her. 'That shrub's not going to hold him for long.' The topic of Dodger's foot was clearly over. 'Luke and Jess, you'll have to stay here with the horses while Grace drives and I lead Muscles out of the window. We'll come back with a truck. Will you be right for a short while?'

What, out here, in the middle of nowhere, in the dark?

'We'll be right,' said Luke, leading Marnie over.

'I'll leave the blue dog here with you,' said Lawson.

The blue puppy, you mean.

'Okay, yeah, that'd be good,' said Jess, trying to sound as confident as Luke.

'Watch out for daisy burrs – they'll put a big hole in your foot. I got a flat tyre on one of them once.'

'Bit late, but thanks.'

'Here, you'd better take a jacket, too,' said Lawson, shaking his head. He pulled off his fleece-lined denim jacket and threw it at Jess. 'Dunno what you thought you were gonna do out here half-dressed.'

Then he retrieved Muscles and jumped in the passenger side of the ute with the window open. 'First gear all the way, Gracie.' He stuck his head out the window. 'And don't let go of that mare, Luke. She cost more than my house.'

Grace started the engine and began bunnyhopping down the track with the stallion trotting obediently behind.

'Watch out for the min min lights!' Lawson sang out as they drove off. He chuckled just like his father.

'The min min what?'

24

JESS WAS SERIOUSLY FREEZING. Her teeth chattered, she couldn't feel her feet and her nose burned. Dodger looked miserable too, standing stiffly in the cold night air. He groaned and let himself down onto his knees, and then dropped heavily onto his side with his legs folded beneath him and his nose resting on the ground.

'It's freezing out here,' said Jess.

'Sure is,' said Luke. He paced around with his shoulders hunched, blowing into his hands to warm them. The mare walked after him.

Jess crouched down next to Dodger and stroked his neck. 'You're a naughty boy for running away, Dodgey.' She rubbed between his ears. 'I'm so glad you didn't hurt yourself.' His fur was deliciously warm under his thick forelock, so she moved closer, and since he didn't seem to mind, crawled up in a ball under his neck with the pup on her lap.

She looked out across the pebbly downs of Longwood. Billions of stars blazed above, all the way to the horizon. The moon, big and bright and beautiful, cast shadows under the gidgea trees. Beyond them, Chelpie grazed alone, glowing white in the moonlight.

It had been her all along. She'd spooked the cattle, the cattle ran through the fences, then Rocko must have hunted Diamond into the grid.

'That's the whitest horse I've ever seen,' said Luke suddenly, snapping her from her thoughts.

'That's because it's *truly white*,' said Jess in a bitter, mimicking voice. 'Not just a *grey* that's faded with *age*.'

Luke groaned. 'She's a pain in the arse, that Katrina, isn't she?'

'I reckon.' Jess thought of Katrina and Tegan, sitting on their horses, acting all sorry about 'What was its name again?' down on the flats after Diamond had been destroyed. They'd even had the hide to sneer at Dodger.

As if reading her mind, Dodger turned his nose around and nuzzled her. He lifted his tail and let out some particularly noisy air, then nickered softly.

Luke laughed. 'Dodger doesn't like her either.'

Dodger groaned as he let out another one.

Jess waved her hand in front of her nose. 'Pwah, Dodgey.' She couldn't help laughing.

'Don't you think it's weird the way the other horses

221

don't like that Chelpie?' said Luke. 'Ever notice how she always grazes on her own?'

'Yep, it's the same with the cattle,' said Jess. 'She's horrible.'

Her mind was whirling. Katrina and Tegan must have seen Diamond in the grid when they went to catch Chelpie. Diamond was in that grid for hours and they just left her for dead.

'She's been made that way,' said Luke. 'They lock her up in a stable all the time so she doesn't get dirty. No wonder she's so sour. I bet she'd be a much nicer horse if she was treated better.'

Beyond a distant thicket of mulgas Jess could make out some sort of lights, hovering above the trees.

'Looks like our ride's here,' she said, pushing away the pup and pulling herself up from the ground.

'Already?' Luke sounded puzzled. 'That's not where the road is.'

The three lights accelerated quickly, travelling much faster than any vehicle could move in that country. They were smooth and silent, unlike anything Jess had ever seen. Then they stopped and hovered about twenty metres from where she and Luke stood.

'What *is* that thing?' she whispered.

'Dunno,' said Luke. He gathered up Marnie's rope

and held her a little closer. 'Easy, girl,' he said, running a hand down her neck.

The three silvery lights shone intensely, illuminating the surrounding trees. They bobbed up and down, whirled around playfully, then sped off towards Chelpie, grazing in the distance.

'What the heck?' Luke whispered. Marnie began pulling at the rope. 'Whoa, girl.' The mare only pulled harder.

'Don't let go of her,' said Jess. 'Lawson'll kill you.'

'I know,' said Luke, holding onto the mare's rope with both hands. 'But . . . I can't hold her!' The mare broke into a trot, pulling the rope through his hands until she jerked free. She trotted over to Chelpie and then put her head down and started grazing.

'Stay here. Don't go after her,' hissed Jess. 'Don't go near those . . .'

What the hell are they?

'Will they hurt her?'

'I don't know.'

Jess glanced down at Dodger, who just lay there with heavy eyelids, looking as though he was about to fall asleep. 'Are you in a coma or something, Dodger? Didn't you see that?'

The pup trotted towards the lights with its hackles up and let out something halfway between a whine and a growl. The lights began to move playfully around Marnie, who just continued grazing. They whizzed under her belly and danced around her head, circling her again and again while she calmly walked over to a mulga bush and nibbled the seedpods off a low-hanging branch. Luke walked after her as though he too were in a trance.

Then without warning the lights zoomed back towards Jess, but rather than hovering at a distance they came right up and began to circle and dance around her. A warm glow radiated from them. Jess stood with her arms outstretched and giggled. The pup yapped around her feet, jumping up and snapping at the air.

All too soon it was over. The lights whizzed back to Marnie, circled her again, and then, as if disappearing into the belly of the mare – blip – they were gone.

25

TAP, TAP. Tap, tap. Tap, tap.

The sounds broke into Jess's sleep. Someone was shoeing a horse outside while she, and indeed the sun, had barely begun to greet the new day. Next to her, Grace and Rosie lay motionless, mops of hair poking out the top of their swags.

Jess looked at her watch. It was all over for her now. The second round of the junior event started in half an hour. There was no way she could win that draft with Dodger's foot in such a mess. She would never own Walkabout. She rolled onto her side.

Lying in her lumpy swag, she thought about the previous night – the warm, bright lights dancing around her, and then disappearing into the belly of the mare. It was as though three stars had fallen out of the sky and come to life. Stanley and Lawson had come back in a borrowed truck to find her and Luke standing stupefied in the dark, gibbering about lights and ghosts and reincarnation.

No one had believed them. People said they were motorbike lights, or gas balls, luminescent insects even. Except for Lawson: he said they were min min lights.

'I camped a big mob of cattle out this way once,' he told them. 'Took 'em until after midnight to settle down and cud. Then this strange light came out of nowhere and danced all over them till I was sure they would up and rush. I thought I was seeing things; thought I'd had too much rum.' He snorted. 'I had some rum *after* I saw it, I can tell ya!'

Jess couldn't help feeling they had something to do with Diamond. Those three silver lights, like shining diamonds, just like her markings.

It must have been her. But what was she trying to say?

Tap, tap. Tap, tap. Clink. A farrier's furnace roared to life outside the window. Jess hopped out to see Lawson tossing a heavy, custom-made shoe into a small gas furnace on the back of his truck. He squeezed Dodger's leg and picked up his injured hoof.

'Lawson?'

'Are you going to hold this old brumby for me, or what?' he said, without looking up. 'I might be able to bridge this with a strap of steel. It's a bit of an old-fashioned method, but I don't have any fancy gear with me. Won't hold forever, but it'll get you through the finals.'

'Will he be in any pain?' asked Jess, taking the rope and giving Dodger a pat.

'Nah, he doesn't seem to have damaged the sole. If this shoe comes off it could be another story, though. He wouldn't want to split that hoof any further.'

Lawson held Dodger's foot in his lap and rummaged in his pocket. He put several tiny screws between his lips, and delved in his tool belt for a power drill. He began to fix a plate over the hole in Dodger's foot.

'You'll have to turn him out to pasture when you get him home, and let it grow back,' he said through the screws in his mouth.

With the plate on it, the hoof looked well and truly fortified. Jess's heart did a little leap inside her chest. She had ranked in the top ten competitors yesterday, and if she could get a good score in the second round, she was in with a real chance.

'If you're not doing anything useful, you could get me a coffee.'

'Uh? Oh, sure.'

'And for Pete's sake, will you put some shoes on?'

Jess dived back into the truck. She squeezed her eyes shut and victory-punched the air. It *was* Diamond. She *was* in the lights. She was telling Jess she would win the draft!

She had to reshuffle her entire brain. 'Boots, boots, where are my boots?' As she scrambled into her clothes, she heard Harry's voice outside. She peeked through the window.

'Your event is on, son. You'd better get that mare saddled up.'

'Yeah, I was supposed to be on half an hour ago,' Lawson mumbled, keeping his head under Dodger. 'Thought I'd fix this kid's horse. She might have a shot at the junior title.'

'But you're in the finals.' Harry glanced at his watch.

'That Jessica kid showed real guts catching that stallion last night. I'm gonna do a quick patch job on her horse's foot and then pack up and go home.'

'How come?' Harry sounded confused.

'The mare's not running right. I scratched her.'

'What's wrong with her?'

'Dunno. She's just not right.'

Jess shrank down below the window so the men couldn't see her, but kept listening.

'She was a bit jumpy yesterday,' Harry offered. 'You wanna warm her up a bit more before the event.'

'It's nothing I can't handle.' Lawson was starting to sound bristly.

'Yeah, righto, I was just trying to help. Seems a shame to miss out on the finals, though.'

'I said, it's nothing I can't handle.'

'Maybe you could use a different bit in her mouth, something a bit softer, a rubber one maybe.'

Lawson let out an exasperated sigh. 'For God's sake, Harry! I said she wasn't right. I'm going to sit this one out!' Jess heard footsteps and a banging of steel over an anvil. 'What do you want me to do? Dope her up, the way your precious stepson does with his horses? She's just not ready yet, so back off.'

There was a silence. Jess wanted to peek out the window again but didn't dare. She crept towards the side door and peered through the crack.

Harry spoke in a guarded but gentle tone. 'Lawson, that was years ago. You need to let go of it, son, move on.'

'I am moving on, Harry. I'm going to shoe this horse and then I'm packing up for home.'

'You're letting it eat you to pieces. You're just not the same person anymore.'

'It's nothing to you that Ryan killed Dusty, is it?'

There was a pause.

'That horse was twenty-five years old, Lawson.'

'Yeah, well, he would've lived to thirty-five if Ryan'd left him alone.'

'He made a mistake,' said Harry. 'I know it was a bad one, but that's what it was – a mistake.'

Lawson's voice rose. 'Well, it wasn't his mistake to

229

make. You don't go sticking a needle into someone else's horse. He killed him! He stuck him so full of dope that Dusty collapsed on me in the middle of an event. And you still treat him same as ever.'

'Lawson, you know I don't agree with what he did. There's no excuse for doping a horse, but you're going to eat yourself up with bitterness if you don't forgive him and get on with life. He didn't mean to kill Dusty. He absolutely idolised you. He just wanted to see you win an event on that old horse. He thought it would make you happy.'

'I didn't want to win an event on that old horse. I just wanted to ride him. And I wanted to see him retired out in a big grassy paddock to live out his days. That's what he deserved. Not to drop dead from an overdose in front of a crowd of people.'

'I know all that, son. But Ryan was a messed-up kid.'

'He's a drunk,' said Lawson with contempt. 'I don't know why you defend him all the time.'

'Because he's family; blood or no blood, he's your brother. You stick by your family, it's unconditional.'

'He's *not* my brother,' snarled Lawson. 'None of these orphans that you want to adopt are my brothers!'

Harry stood there a moment longer, then said, 'I don't even know who you are anymore.' He turned and walked away.

Lawson turned around and saw Jess in the doorway of the truck, dumbstruck.

'Are you going to get me a coffee or what?' he snapped. He threw his tools into a bucket with a loud clatter.

Jess scurried back into the truck.

Dodger cantered around the outside of the arena. He felt as sound as a bell and seemed not at all tired by the events of the previous night. As the announcer called her name, Jess brought him back to a walk and took her place in the line outside the camp. In the stands, Caroline and Craig waved madly, oblivious to the night's adventures. Hetty and Aunt Margaret sat next to them, eating burgers.

This is it. Stay with me, Diamond.

She eyed the cattle. A motley lot of mixed breeds hustled to the back of the yard while a girl on a flashy palomino charged out the gate after one of them. Next was a boy on a grey stockhorse. He scored a cut-out of twenty-two, but sailed past the beast at the first peg.

Then it was Jess's turn. She entered the camp, running her eyes over the cattle. A big, cumbersome steer took her fancy. It ambled about in the centre of the mob, looking alert and ready to flee. It was perfect. Nice and big and fast.

'You just wait there, Missy, while we change the cattle over. This lot need a drink. We'll get you a fresh lot, ay.'

Damn!

Two men in big hats chased the cattle out the gate and set about bringing a fresh mob in through the yards.

'You see a min min light?' the stockman suddenly asked her.

'Yes, I did, how did you know?'

'Lawson's a friend of mine. He told me.'

'There were three of them and they just disappeared into one of the mares. Why? Have you seen them too?'

'Oh yeah, seen it a couple of times. Pretty spooky, ay? Never seen three at the same time, though.' He shook his head, a grim look on his face.

'What are they?'

He squinted and whispered in a low voice, 'Ghosts, *debil debil*. You wanna stay away from that mare, Missy.' Then he swung the gate open for her. 'Cattle are up.'

Stay away from Marnie?

Jess focused on the cattle.

In the yard more of the same mixed breeds milled about. She walked around and had a good look at them. She exchanged glances with the judge, then approached the mob.

A plain black Angus trotted down the side of the

fence, bellowing like an old man. He was big and agitated, with clear purpose in his stride.

'You're mine, sucker!'

Jess snuck in behind, easily pushing the steer away from the others. It bolted down to the front of the camp and turned its head about, as though searching. A lovesick moo floated across the arena. The beast immediately turned, rammed its head through the big steel gates and bellowed back. It stamped its front foot at the ground and pushed at the gates, nearly lifting them off their hinges.

Jess legged Dodger from side to side, wondering how to get the animal's head out of the metal bars. She trotted Dodger up and gave it a nudge. '*Hah!*'

It turned and eyeballed her without pulling its head out of the gate, then gazed longingly across the arena. It wailed again. A cow bellowed back.

'Hah!' Jess yelled, reining Dodger back and forth. '*HAH!*'

The steer ignored her. It continued to exchange wails with its lovesick friend. Jess pushed Dodger up closer and gave it another nudge. It kicked out with a hind leg but didn't move. A muffled giggle went through the crowd.

She tried whistling at it. The steer clamped its tail between its legs and closed its eyes.

She couldn't believe it. It was in love!

She rode up and gave it another nudge, harder this time. 'Move it, Romeo!'

A roar of laughter went through the crowd. There were whistles and yells.

She came around and gave the steer a good shove on the other side. It pushed its head deeper into the gate. The clock was ticking. She had no choice. '*Gate!*'

The stockman released the gates and the cow wrestled its head out from between the panels. As she followed it into the main arena she could just hear the judge above the laughter of the crowd. He called a cut-out score of thirteen.

Jess would have to complete the course in breakneck speed to make up the points. She set out after the steer, which trotted in a dead straight line towards the herd at the other end of the arena.

Dodger leaned heavily against its shoulder, pushing with all his power to get the beast to turn. But it was single-minded, slowly bulldozing forward. Dodger set his ears back and gnashed his teeth. He tossed his head.

Jess yelled, '*HAH!*'

She heard the crack of the judge's whip.

Eliminated?

She brought Dodger back. He pranced around, not yet ready to let the beast go.

She couldn't believe it.

Neither she nor Dodger had done anything particularly wrong, but the beast was just a dud. A total dud. Jess gave Dodger a pat on the neck and dropped the reins.

The crowd were on their feet, clapping, but that was it. Her attempt to save Walkabout was over.

Finished.

26

JESS HEADED FOR the horse wash, Dodger puffing behind her. The announcer's rambling monologue followed them, and Jess wished he would just shut up.

Dodger took long cool gulps of water from his bucket, and Jess watched them travel up and along his gullet. She looked at his robotic hoof. It was ridiculous. How could she have believed that Diamond was speaking to her?

Me, win a campdraft? She laughed out loud.

'What's funny?'

Jess spun around and saw Luke, holding Legsy by the halter. He took the hose and began filling a bucket.

'Everything,' said Jess. 'Those lights. I thought they were spirits. I thought it was Diamond.'

'I can't stop thinking about them,' said Luke.

'They were probably just balls of gas.'

'Yeah, probably.' Luke still sounded uneasy.

They both stood there, letting their horses drink. In

the distance Tegan Broadhead picked out Chelpie's hooves while Katrina sat on a fold-out chair and sipped from a can of lemonade. 'I'm going to win the Best in Show trophy, I know it,' Jess heard Katrina say. 'Chelpie is by far the best horse here.'

'Chelpie is by far the biggest troublemaker here,' Jess muttered to Luke.

'Lawson wants to put a bullet in her,' said Luke.

Jess thought about Lawson and Dusty. It had never occurred to her that someone like him could have gone through the same thing as her, losing their first horse. She thought about the anger Lawson carried around inside.

'Shara is on in the finals soon,' said Luke.

'Yeah, I know,' said Jess. She ran her hand over Dodger's back. There was one thing she needed to do before she packed up to go home. 'I have to go and talk to her.' She pulled Dodger's head up out of the bucket. 'Come on, Dodge.'

She led him to the side of the nearby horse float, where Shara was brushing Rocko's rump.

'I found out how Diamond got out, Shara.'

Shara continued brushing Rocko and didn't look up. 'How?'

'It wasn't Rocko's fault.'

Shara stopped brushing for a moment. 'No kidding.'

'Lawson Blake—'

'I knew it was him!' Shara brushed Rocko with hard, sharp strokes.

'No, listen to me, Shara. Lawson's been seeing Katrina's horse loose down by the river. You know, Chelpie. The other horses hate her. She gets them so worked up. I don't know what it is about her.'

'I wouldn't believe anything that Lawson says.' Shara slung the brush into a bag by the float. 'Reality check, Jessica. Look what he did to your face when he let off that gunshot!' She threw her saddle over Rocko's back and yanked the saddlecloth up through the gullet.

'He thought we'd been stirring up his cattle. Don't you see?' said Jess. 'He knew something was bothering his stock, but he didn't know what. When he saw us down there, he just assumed it was us. But it was *Chelpie*. Chelpie must have chased the cattle straight through the electric fence. That's how the horses got out.'

Shara was silent as she tightened her girth.

'I should have talked to you. I'm really sorry, Shara.'

'I bet you anything Chelpie chased Diamond through that grid, not Rocko,' said Shara.

'But didn't you see Rocko do it?'

Shara shook her head. 'No, I didn't. No one saw it happen. I just assumed it was him because he had been chasing her that morning. But what was chasing *him*, Jess? Why was he so stirred up? He knew Diamond, they

238

travelled together every weekend. He wouldn't chase her that far, not for a whole mile down the river. Diamond would've just turned around and kicked at him.'

Shara was right, Diamond had never been frightened of Rocko. Only people were frightened of Rocko.

'Katrina knew,' said Jess slowly. 'She set us up against each other. I bet she even saw it happen. She started the rumours about Rocko.'

'Greasy low-life,' said Shara, putting on her helmet. 'I have to go warm up.' As she rode away, she turned back to Jess. 'This one's for Diamond, Jessy.'

Jess walked over to the arena and joined Tom and Rosie on the top rail of the fence. There were only two riders left to go before Shara, who sat with her long legs relaxed against the fenders of the saddle. She wore a pale blue shirt and her hair was neatly plaited. Rocko gleamed, looking powerful and fit.

Questions hammered in Jess's brain. Who did Shara ride with these days? Who taught her to draft? Did she have new friends now? From her new school?

Jess felt she didn't know anything about Shara anymore. But she wanted to. She wanted to know everything, the way she used to. If it wasn't her destiny to win the draft, then it would be awesome if Shara did.

'Come on, Jessy,' said Rosie, shifting her bum along to let Jess in. Jess wrestled a leg over the fence and tried to make room for Grace, who squeezed in beside her and linked elbows.

The rails were full of people watching the finals. In the camp, cattle bellowed while stockmen whistled and yelled and slapped their rumps as gates opened and closed. The announcer still prattled on, organising competitors, announcing scores and thanking sponsors.

Luke appeared suddenly under Jess's armpit. Jess tried to move along a bit. But Grace quickly moved to fill the space. 'There's no room,' she said. Luke scowled, hopped down and resurfaced under Tom's elbow further down.

'No need to fight, guys,' said Rosie.

'Your friend's going to be rich if she wins this, Jess,' said Tom. 'Reckon she'd buy Wally for you?'

'I wouldn't ask her to,' Jess said.

Shara guided Rocko through the gate. Inside the camp, she faced up to the cattle and ducked back and forth a few times. The mob huddled at the back of the yard and eyed her nervously, while she studied each beast. She spun Rocko away from them and stopped abruptly to face the judge. They exchanged nods and she spun back to the cattle.

Shara approached the mob, and cleanly and precisely cut out a lanky black steer. It frolicked playfully to the front of the yard, then tried to dart back to the other cattle. Shara spun Rocko and galloped two quick strides to block it. The steer skidded to a halt, mooed loudly and tried to duck around in the other direction. Rocko pivoted neatly on his hocks and galloped ahead to thwart it. The steer darted back and forth, desperately trying to find a gap, but Rocko had it covered, block by block pushing him closer to the front of the yard. Shara yelled for the gates.

The yard men swung them open and a cheer erupted from the stands. Rosie clamped a hand on Jess's leg and squeezed it tight. 'Wow! What a cut-out!' she squealed.

The steer burst out and Rocko exploded after it. Shara gave him his head, reining him out wide and driving the beast in a big loop around the first peg. She galloped up on its shoulder as it headed towards the cattle that remained in the yards, yelling at it to keep moving. As it bleated to the herd behind the gates, Rocko gave it a shove with his shoulder and herded it towards the next peg. It took off again, swishing its tail and kicking out with its hind legs. Shara raced after it, bringing it around the second peg in another big, tidy loop.

The crowd stood up in the stands. Jess jumped to her feet and screamed. '*Go, Shara!*'

Shara threw the reins at Rocko and he shifted into overdrive, thundering up behind the beast, forcing it into a U-turn back up and between the two finish pegs. As it ducked through the pegs, Rocko's legs skidded madly to make the turn behind it. Shara's balance shifted suddenly and her stirrup flew out from the saddle, landing metres behind her. But she didn't miss a beat. She sat deep in the saddle and swerved with Rocko as they scrambled through the two white finishing poles.

The grandstand went silent. All eyes shifted to the man on the ageing grey stockhorse, as they waited for him to call the score. Jess didn't breathe. The judge lifted his head.

'Twenty-two for cut-out,' he called, then paused to let the scorers jot that down, 'and sixty for horse work.' He paused again. 'Four for the course.'

The grandstand began to murmur, people calculated out loud. The announcer finally called it: 'That's our last competitor in the Junior Draft and it's also our winner, folks. Shara Wilson has it with a score of eighty-six on top of a score yesterday of eighty-two. That's an impressive total of *one hundred and sixty-eight!*'

Jessica jumped off the fence and into the camp with the cattle. '*HAH!*' she yelled at them, sending them to the back of the yard. She squeezed through the gate panels, into the arena and ran out to the finish poles.

She spotted the stirrup, grabbed it and dusted it off on her jeans. In front of her, Shara loosened the reins and walked Rocko towards her. Both horse and rider blew heavily.

Jess held out the stirrup. 'That was amazing, Sharsy!'

A smile spread across Shara's lovely moon-face; a smile that could light up a midnight sky. 'Thanks, Sis,' she said, breathlessly.

My buddy, my bestie – you're back!

Shara took the stirrup and fumbled around under her leg, clipping it back onto the saddle. Rocko fidgeted around, flicking his ears back and forth and chewing at the bit. He almost looked happy.

Jess reached out and gave him a couple of slaps on his neck. He was hot and damp with sweat. 'You're a good boy, Rocko,' she said, then took a step back as he flattened his ears and screwed up his nose at her.

Shara laughed and threw her arms around his neck. 'I knew you could do it, Rocko. You're a good horse. I don't care what anyone says.'

'Are you two going to do a lap of honour or are you gonna stand there smooching all day?' Jess asked.

'You bet,' said Shara. She lifted her reins and gave Rocko a kick. 'Watch this!'

Jess stood alone in the arena. She smiled as Shara cantered past the crowd and waved to them.

Oh, she's not . . .

Shara turned Rocko in a big circle and brought him past the crowd again. As she approached the grandstand, she dropped her reins and waved to the crowd with both hands. Then as she passed them, she swung one leg over the front of the saddle and sat sideways to face them, both arms in the air, waving. As she departed, she swung her leg over Rocko's rump to face backwards, still facing the crowd, waving as Rocko cantered away from them. The crowd roared with laughter and gave her a standing ovation.

Jess shook her head and rolled her eyes. Shara always did love to show off.

Shara swung her legs around and sat forward in the saddle. Then she made a beeline for Jess, leaned out of her saddle and held out an arm.

Jess laughed and put her arm up ready for the grab. Their arms collided and locked in a tight grip. She took a quick step forward and swung up behind Shara onto Rocko's rump. Jess felt Shara's legs kicking and Rocko burst into a gallop. She put both arms in the air and screamed out loud, 'Woohoo!'

'Riders, please be aware that juniors are not permitted to ride without helmets. Please dismount immediately or you will be disqualified. I repeat, please dismount immediately or you will be disqualified.'

'That announcer just never shuts up!'

'Don't worry about it, you're disqualified anyway,' laughed Shara as she pulled Rocko back to a walk.

'Yeah, but you're not,' said Jess. 'Better let me off or you'll lose fifteen hundred bucks!'

'Will that rider please dismount,' called the announcer again. 'I repeat, will that rider please dismount and leave the arena.'

'Yeah, yeah, give us a chance,' said Shara as she pulled Rocko to a halt. 'Some people just have no sense of humour.'

As Jess slipped off Rocko's rump, she said, 'I'm so glad you're here, Sharsy.'

Shara brought Rocko around to face her. She grinned. 'You wanna know the funniest thing?'

'What?'

'I took up campdrafting so I wouldn't have to run into you!'

'*Heyyy!*'

'Riders, will you please leave the arena,' called the announcer again.

'Oh, all *right!*' said Shara. 'I'd better go before he blows a gasket,' she said to Jess.

'When you get Rocko hosed off, come over to our truck. You absolutely *have* to meet my new friends,' said Jess.

'Who's the boy?' grinned Shara.

'Hey?'

'The redhead.'

'What redhead?'

'The one that can't take his eyes off you, der.'

'What are you on about?'

Shara just shrugged and gave her a knowing look.

Jess changed the subject. 'You have to meet Gracie!' She grinned and said in a teasing voice. 'She's my *new* bestie!'

'Oh, is she now?' laughed Shara as she rode away. She looked back over her shoulder and called out, 'But is she your *best* bestie?'

'Will that person on foot please leave the arena immediately,' called the announcer again. He was beginning to sound cranky. 'There are cattle loose in the arena!'

Jess saw a huge red bull clambering over the rails with half a dozen stockmen waving and shouting at it. It rolled over the top of the fence, landed on its side in the arena with an ungraceful thud, and then scrambled to its feet.

'Holy . . .' Jess began running to a fence as the bull spotted her. It lowered its head and charged.

'Someone get the gate!' a person yelled, too late.

The bull trotted through the open gateway, and into the show arena. Jess hauled herself onto the rail and watched it canter blindly through bunting and tents as several stockmen gave chase. People scattered and horses shied.

In the centre arena, Katrina Pettilow stood in the winners' line waiting for her Best in Show trophy. As the judge approached with the gleaming golden cup and a satin sash, Katrina leaned across and held out her arms, smiling proudly.

Chelpie snorted and began to shift about. Then, like a stack of dominos, the line-up of horses scattered in all directions as a bull and twenty stockmen came galloping towards them. Katrina clung to Chelpie's pure white neck while the pony bolted from the arena. The judge dropped the trophy and ran, leaving it to be trampled by the bull and its chasers.

27

AS SHE ROLLED UP swags and packed away buckets and saddles, Jess saw a big golden cut-out trophy sitting on the fold-out table in the back of the truck. She smiled and looked out the window, searching for Harry. She saw Ryan drive into the grounds. On the back of his ute, a rotund figure on four legs balanced precariously, snorting and grunting noisily. Biyanga heard the commotion, and let out a shrill whinny from where he was tethered at the truck.

'Grunter!' Jess called out in delight. 'Grace! Rosie! Grunter's here!'

Grunter stomped around noisily, freaking out several horses when he paraded past as though he were on a Mardi Gras float. He was huge. In three months he'd doubled in size.

Harry came limping out from between two trucks. 'Well, I'll be jiggered,' he chuckled.

Ryan leaned out the window of the vehicle. 'He turned up in Mum's veggie patch yesterday. She said if I didn't get him out of there, she'd put him in the freezer.'

'We can't let that happen,' grinned Harry, as he pulled down the back of the ute.

Jess watched as Harry led the pig over to Biyanga. The two buddies grunted and snuffled each other for a few minutes before Grunter found his way to the feedbin. She smiled and continued to pack up her gear.

From the corner of her eye she saw Lawson. He glared at Ryan and then turned his back to talk to a man in a big black hat. Jess recognised him as the man in the camp who had asked her about the min min lights. They began walking towards her.

She kept packing, pretending she didn't see them.

'Hey, Jess,' said Lawson.

'Hi Lawson.' She nodded at the stockman. 'Hello.'

'Bob,' he said, holding out a hand to shake.

She wiped her hand on her jeans and shook it as she had seen her father do when he met other men. 'Hi, I'm Jess.'

'Lawson reckons you might sell that gelding for the right price,' said Bob. 'He says you've got your eye on a good filly back home. My boy needs a good horse to learn drafting on and I don't reckon he'd get any better than old Dodger.'

Jess stared at Lawson in surprise. 'But don't you want to buy Walkabout?'

'Bob's a mate of mine, Jess. He's got a nine-year-old son who's a pretty handy young rider and helps work the cattle around the yards at home. Dodger would have to work the yards and then draft on weekends.' Lawson gave her a nod. 'He'd get a pretty comfortable retirement when the kid outgrows him too.'

'I couldn't sell him for less than two thousand dollars,' said Jess in a dismissive tone. No one in their right mind would pay that much money for Dodger. She ran her eyes over her horse: a twenty-two-year-old station-bred gelding with a remarkably ugly head and a badly busted-up foot. He lifted his tail, did a large poo and ripped at his hay with an already over-full mouth.

'Sounds like a fair price,' said the stockman. 'I see a lotta horses go through them yards, and there's not many as good as Dodger. I've watched him for years, ay.'

Jess was astounded. It was too easy. Two thousand dollars was enough to buy Walkabout. It was the whole reason she had come to the draft. All she had to do was say yes.

This guy was actually going to give her two thousand dollars. She could have Walkabout.

But it meant losing Dodger . . .

'Can I have some time to think about it?'

'Sure. You tell Lawson when you make up your mind. No hurry,' said Bob. 'He's a top little horse, that one, and we'd give him a good home.' He turned to Lawson. 'Thanks for the intro, mate. Catch up later, hey?'

Jess watched him walk away and then stared at Dodger again. He had become so special to her. He was no longer her cousin's horse. He was her horse; her buddy, who she had come to know and trust.

You're worth two million to me, Dodgey.

'What's the matter? Can't part with the old fella?' Lawson put his hands in his pockets and stared at her. 'Come over here. I want to talk to you.' He walked over to the truck, sat on the tailgate and patted the floor next to him. 'Bob's right about that horse. His type is real hard to come by. He's honest, experienced and tough as old boots. You've still got a lot of days ahead of you on that horse, Jess.'

'But what about Wally? I'd have more days with her.' Jess was arguing with herself as much as Lawson.

Lawson rubbed his chin and was quiet for a moment.

'You want her for yourself,' she said.

Lawson nodded. 'Yep.' He nodded again. 'Yep, I do. I'll admit that.' He turned to her. 'But you do too, from what I've heard.'

Jess was silent.

'Hey?' He pushed her for an answer.

'You're going to think I'm really stupid, but Walkabout was born on the same day as my first horse died. Diamond died under a coachwood tree and Walkabout was born under a coachwood tree. I sort of feel Walkabout was *meant* for me. It's spooky.'

Lawson laughed. 'Did the old man spin you that yarn about ancestral spirits?'

'Yeah, he did. Why? Do you think it's crap?' She tried to gauge his thoughts.

'No, not at all. But you've twisted it all around, Jess. I know you're just trying to make sense of things, but totems aren't about reincarnation. They're about story and kin. They're about how people place themselves in the world. It's serious business. You shouldn't go messing with it like that.'

Jess sighed and stared at her shoes.

'Jess, at some time, everybody loses their first horse. Every rider in the country has memories of their first horse, even world champions. They're special. They're the ones that are the hardest of all to let go.'

'You ought to know.'

'Yeah, old Dusty.' He picked a piece of hay off the floor he was sitting on and played around with it thoughtfully. 'Dad caught a brumby mare down in the Snowy Mountains. She was the first brumby he ever caught. She was a feral old thing, wild as. I called her Frosty because she was white as snow.'

Jess laughed. 'She wasn't *truly* white, was she?'

'Stuffed if I know.' He chuckled. 'She was just a feral brumby. But I wanted her so bad. The old man said she was too old to break in and train. So he let me have her first foal.'

'Dusty,' said Jess.

'Yep. I thought he was the most handsome horse I'd ever seen when I was a kid. I had him for nearly twenty years. He always had something wild and untamed about him. He was his own person, if you know what I mean. He could really work. He'd muster all day without a drink and all he'd want in return was a loose rein and a feed at the end of the day. He'd chase cattle till he dropped.' Lawson made small circles in the dust of the tailgate with the piece of straw. 'Wasn't much chop at campdrafts though; he'd get too jumpy.' His voice trailed off and his tone changed. His eyes wandered over to the stables where Ryan talked with Harry.

'It's bad when you lose them, isn't it?'

'Yep,' said Lawson.

'I blamed my best friend for killing Diamond. I was really bad to her.'

'Yeah, I heard the two of you screeching like a pair of

galahs down on the river flats that day.' He looked at her and winced. 'Sorry about your face.'

'It really hurt, you know.'

'Yeah, I bet it did.'

'It didn't hurt as much as losing my best friend, though.'

Lawson glanced at Ryan and his jaw set hard. 'He has *never* been a friend, if that's what you're getting at.' Then he snorted. 'At least he's sober today.'

'Reckon you'll ever forgive him?'

'No,' said Lawson in a hard voice. Then he changed the subject. 'So what's your decision? You gonna sell *your* old brumby?'

Jess was still torn. 'Tell me why you want Walkabout.'

'She's my once-in-a-lifetime horse, Jess. I know you have a really close connection with her but I reckon she's meant for big things. Every rider at some stage in his life comes across a special horse. Like Dad has Biyanga. She is meant for me, Jess, I know it.'

Jess stared at him. If only she could believe him . . .

'Why were you so cruel to her?'

Lawson looked at her puzzled. 'Hey?'

'Down in the mares' paddock that day. You threw her to the ground and gave her rope burns. You and another guy. I saw you.'

Lawson went quiet and ran his tongue along his lips as

he thought. 'Oh yeah, that,' he said, scratching the back of his neck uncomfortably. 'She had an infection in her navel. We were putting iodine on it.'

Oh yeah, that?

Jess just stared at him, incredulous that he could be so indifferent.

He stared back. 'What?'

'You hurt her and you scared her.'

'Jess, foals get really sick with infected navels. She would have died if we hadn't treated it.'

'You still didn't have to rope her. She would have let me put it on without even a halter.'

'Yeah, well, how was I to know you were some sort of filly whisperer?' he said, shaking his head with a faint smile. 'I had the owner there and it was he who roped her, I might point out. He was livid that the filly's cord hadn't been cleaned. Usually the old man puts iodine on as soon as they're born, but she went missing for a few days, he reckons.'

'But you helped him. I saw you.'

'Well, if you reckon you can handle her without ropes and do a better job, you can break her in when she's ready. How's that for a deal?'

'I've never taught a horse to be ridden before.'

'Then the filly can be your first. I'll show you how.'

Jess just looked at him.

'Oh, that's right,' said Lawson. 'You're the filly whisperer. You probably want to show me.' He laughed.

'So, what about Marnie?'

Lawson groaned as though remembering something unpleasant. 'She's probably knocked up after that rendezvous with Muscles last night. I'll have to get a vet out to her to give her a needle before it's too late. I don't want some mongrel-bred foal from that rogue stallion added to my feed bill.'

Jess ran her hands through her hair and sighed. 'Why does life have to be so complicated?'

'Why don't you take some time to think about it,' said Lawson. 'I'll give you my number. If you really are willing to sell that old stockhorse, then give me a ring. I'll back off and let you buy Walkabout.'

'And if I can't sell him?'

'The filly's mine.'

28

JESS SAT UNDER the trees in the mares' paddock. Walkabout snuffled her head and breathed puffy kisses over her cheeks. She smiled. 'You're so cute, Wally.'

'Hey, Jess.'

She spun around. Luke had a halter in his hand.

'You've come to get her, haven't you?'

He nodded.

Jess looked to the ground.

Luke slipped through the fence and sat down next to her. 'You'll still be able to see her all the time, and break her in one day.'

'I feel like I've let her down.'

'Nah, you haven't. You don't have to own her to have that bond with her. Connecting with a horse isn't about owning it.'

'Reckon?'

'You already proved it.' He shrugged. 'I can't afford to

buy Legsy either, but he'll always be *my* mate. Harry'll never have the same bond with him that I do.'

'Can't you save up for Legsy? All those ribbons and prizes you win. You'd have a much better chance than me.' Luke and Legs had won the working stockhorse class at the draft and knocked off half the open riders. Jess was only just beginning to realise what a good rider he was.

'Every time I win a class on him, his value goes up.' Luke laughed at the irony. 'I get to ride him. That's good enough for me.'

'At least you don't have to worry about Lawson buying him,' she said.

'No, he'll just inherit him.'

Jess laughed. 'He'd have to kill Harry off first.'

Luke looked down and picked at some grass. 'Harry's got lung cancer, Jess.'

Jess's face dropped. 'Hey?'

'Lawson will get Legs. One day.'

'Harry's got *cancer*?'

'It's not real bad,' said Luke. 'Harry'll fight it. He'll be around for ages yet.'

'It's still terrible.'

'He's a tough old fella,' said Luke, as though trying to convince himself as much as Jess. He looked up and tried to smile. 'Take more than that to knock him around.'

'Wouldn't he leave you Legsy?'

'Lawson's blood, Ryan's adopted, I'm fostered,' he said, explaining the hierarchy again. 'There'll be enough fighting over Biyanga without me putting my hand up for Legsy.'

Jess was stunned. 'So Lawson's going to get *both* our horses?'

'Lawson's all right,' said Luke. 'He's pretty good with his own horses. Doesn't fuss over them much, but he's fair.'

'He won't care about them the way we do, you know he won't.'

'Maybe not,' Luke shrugged. 'Maybe yes, but in a different way. Harry reckons he was nuts about that horse, Dusty. He's pretty fussy about what happens to Marnie, too.'

'He wasn't too happy about her getting pregnant.' Jess couldn't help but giggle.

Luke grinned. 'He freaked.'

Jess thought of Muscles grunting over Marnie, and the min min lights dancing around her belly while she nibbled on mulga seeds. Suddenly her heart skipped a beat.

'Oh, Luke!' She stood up. '*Luke!*'

'What?' He looked at her as though she'd gone kooky.

'The lights! The three white lights!'

'The min min lights?'

'Bob said they were ghosts!'

'Thought you said they were just gas balls?'

'Do *you* reckon they were gas balls?'

'I reckon they were weird.'

'Diamond got her name because she had three silver diamonds on her rump. When the three lights were circling around me I thought it was her, giving me a message, telling me I would win the campdraft.' She rolled her eyes. 'Yeah, I know, that didn't happen.'

'So?'

She lowered her voice. 'Do you reckon they could have been Diamond's spirit? Her ghost? They disappeared into Marnie's belly – *while she was eating mulga seeds!*'

'Mulga seeds?'

'I planted mulga seeds on Diamond's grave! My auntie sent them to me,' Jess grinned at him, 'from Longwood!'

Luke looked totally baffled.

'Reckon Lawson would sell me Marnie's foal?'

'No.'

'Why not?'

'Because the vet's coming this morning to give her a needle.'

'Oh my God, I have to stop him!'

She tore her phone from her pocket.

'Lawson!'

'Jess. You haven't changed your mind, have you?'

'Yes – well, no . . . well, kind of. Has the vet been yet?'

'He's here now. Why?'

'Don't do it. I want the foal. Can I buy the foal?' She paused. 'Please?'

'I don't even know if she's pregnant. She's getting a needle just in case.'

'Lawson, please don't give her that needle. It's the min min!'

'What are you on about now?'

'Diamond got her name because she had three silver diamonds on her rump. There were three min mins, that night at Longwood. They disappeared into Marnie's belly, while she was eating mulga seeds!'

'What?'

'I planted mulga seeds on Diamond's grave! They were from Longwood!'

There was a long silence on the other end of the phone. Jess imagined the faces he was pulling.

'Are you back on that totem trip again?'

'Umm,' Jess thought about it. She was, she definitely was. 'Yes,' she said.

'Girls and bloody horses,' she heard him groan. 'Jess,

I don't know what you're on about, but you shouldn't go getting all excited about something that may not have happened. I don't even know if she's really pregnant.'

'She is. I *know* she is. I have two hundred and forty-six dollars. I'll buy the foal from you.'

'Oh, forget it. She's my good mare,' said Lawson. 'If she had a foal, it'd put her out of action for eleven months. Plus another six months until the foal is weaned.'

'You can still ride her for about six or seven months, so it would really only be about a year,' she corrected him. 'Less, even.'

'Nup,' said Lawson.

'Well, I'll just have to sell Dodger and buy Walkabout, then. You promised me first option, remember.'

'Yeah, but— but . . .' Lawson stammered. 'This is crazy. Are you blackmailing me?'

'Not really,' she grinned. 'I'm doing you a favour. You get your once-in-a-lifetime horse and I get mine.'

Lawson gave a defeatist sigh. 'I'll get the mare tested.'

When she snapped her phone shut, she noticed Luke staring at her. 'What?' She couldn't get the smile off her face.

'You just got a foal out of Marnie for two hundred bucks?'

'Ahuh.'

'Can you ring him back and ask if I can have Legsy for two hundred bucks?'

She shoved him on the shoulder. 'Don't be silly.'

29

JESS HALTERED THE MARE and led her through the gate with Wally frolicking behind. Part of the agreement with Lawson was that she could do all the handling and training until Wally was broken in, and to Jess's way of thinking that included delivering her to his place.

Luke held the gate open for her.

'Watch out for the min mins,' he called, as she led the mare out onto the river flats and then a well-worn track.

She laughed. 'Don't worry, I will!'

She wasn't far along the river flats when she heard a loud 'Coo–ee!'

'Coo–ee!' she called back.

Shara trotted Rocko out from a track running along-side the river and waved. Jess waited for her to get closer and then held out an arm and vaulted onto Rocko's back. With one hand on Shara's waist and the other on the mare's lead, they set off across the flats with Wally following close behind.

They rode along the open flats where the tree-lined river wove through the valley. Some sections of the river flowed slowly and serenely and in other places it rushed through narrow, choking channels. As it meandered back and forth across the flats, the girls crossed through the water, travelling under the trees where it was cool and shady for long stretches.

They stood and let the horses drink, while the dogs rolled about in the sandy patches and lay on their bellies in the cool water, panting happily. Jess closed her eyes and let the trickling sounds of the river flow over her. For a brief moment Rocko was still. She sat there with her eyes closed, with her best friend, listening to the river. A warm puff of air, like the breath of a sleepy horse, ran up the back of her neck.

Hey, Diamond.

'Here come Rosie and Grace!' said Shara.

In the trees along the river, the sound of Rosie and Grace arguing became louder and louder.

'What is *with* those two?' asked Shara.

'Sisters always fight,' said Jess. 'Didn't you know that?'

Shara grinned. 'So do besties.'

Jess grinned back. 'Especially best besties.'

'We just rode past Lawson's place,' said Grace, as she drew up on a chestnut horse Jess had never seen before.

'He said to tell you his mare is pregnant,' said Rosie.

Jess grinned. 'Thought she might be.'

The two sisters looked at her, puzzled.

'Tell you later,' said Jess, fizzing with happiness.

The four girls continued along the river, ducking under branches, jumping over fallen trees and splashing through the water. They cantered across the flats, past the old sawmill and along Slaughtering Creek, where the old cattle grid hid slyly beneath the long grass. They thundered past the Pettilows' place, where Chelpie grazed peacefully, looking impossibly beautiful. The little white mare didn't look up, and for once none of the horses spooked or shied.

'You're a mystery, Chelpie,' Jess said out loud. 'What is it about you?'

When they got to Lawson's place, Jess unbuckled the mare's halter and let her out into the big paddock. Wally trotted alongside her mother for a few strides, then back to Jess, giving her a gentle shove with her nose.

'It's okay, little one, you go and make some new friends. I'll come back and see you tomorrow.'

She watched Wally and her mum sniff the ground and wander into their new surroundings. Then she scanned the paddock, looking for Marnie.

Where is she?

Three other mares stood under a big old mango tree, swishing their tails at the flies. They lifted their heads towards the newcomers. A short way off, Marnie grazed contentedly.

And I'll be back to see you too.

Acknowledgements

Sincere thanks to Tex Skuthorpe and Anne Morrill
for your advice.

Thanks also to my Dad, for your help
and encouragement.

And thanks to my favourite farrier, Pete Salter,
for helping me fix Dodger's foot!

About the Author

KAREN WOOD has been involved with horses for more than twenty years. After owning many horses, she has finally found her once-in-a-lifetime-horse in a little chestnut stockhorse called Reo. Karen has an Arts degree majoring in communications and a diploma in horticulture. She has syndicated a gardening column in several newspapers throughout Australia, has published feature articles in various magazines and has published photographs in bushwalking guides. She is married with two children and lives on the Central Coast, New South Wales.

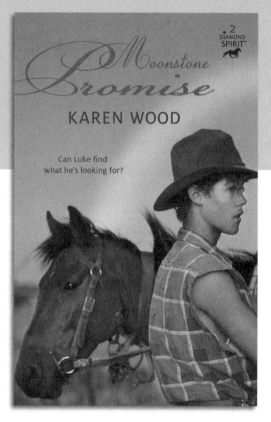

A SNEAK PREVIEW

OF THE SECOND BOOK IN THE DIAMOND SPIRIT SERIES

'LAST ONE!' yelled Tom, as he sent a bale of prime lucerne tumbling off the back of the semitrailer.

Luke let it fall to the ground end-first. It bounced, then toppled onto its side with a thud. He stabbed his hay hooks into it and with one last surge of energy heaved it up to the top of the stack, where Lawson was arranging the bales tightly in a crisscross pattern.

'That it?' yelled Lawson.

'Yep,' Luke shouted back, hanging the hooks onto the beam that ran along the wall of the shed. He was dripping with sweat, itchy from the tiny stalks and dust, and his muscles ached, but he felt great. 'That oughta keep their bellies full for a while,' he said, looking up at the mountain of hay.

Lawson scrambled down the side of the stack like a mountain goat and brushed the loose green leaves from the front of his shirt. 'Eight hundred bales. I'm knackered!'

'Chuck us the water bottle, Luke.' Tom let himself down onto the edge of the empty trailer and sat with his legs hanging over.

Luke tossed a bottle to him, and looked around for a broom. He swept the loose hay into a pile, then leaned on the rake while he looked around the hay shed.

It had taken the three of them all weekend to empty it out for the hay. There'd been stacks of old tyres, drums of diesel, old snigging chains and the skeletal remains of a vintage car. Beneath that they'd found rags, dead mice and mounds of composted God-only-knew-what. They'd salvaged anything worthy, taken the rest to the tip, shovelled up the rotting remains and pressure-hosed the concrete floor. In its place stood the proud castle of leafy green lucerne, enough to last the winter.

Luke got back to sweeping. The sooner he could get this cleaned up, the sooner he could go and find Harry. The old man had been looking brighter this morning. He might even come and do the afternoon feeds. There was a tonne of things Luke wanted Harry to look at down the paddock. He wanted to show him that filly's leg and ask what he wanted done with the western fence.

'Hey, Luke!' Tom's yell from outside stopped him in his tracks. 'Luke, quick! The stallion's out!'

Luke dropped the broom and ran around the side of

the truck. He'd been the last person to go into Biyanga's yard, but couldn't have left the gate unlatched; he was meticulous about that sort of thing. He stopped and glanced around quickly for Harry's good stallion.

Everything was at peace. The mares were grazing, Grunter the pig snuffled at a leaky water trough and chooks pecked busily beneath feed bins. All seemed to be as it should at Harry's place. So what was Tom talking about?

Luke looked up towards the stables and a blast of water hit him with so much force it nearly knocked him over. His arms flew up to shield his face and he stumbled backwards, coughing and spluttering while the jets of water hammered him all over.

Tom screamed with laughter and kept blasting him.

'You're *dead*, Tommo!' Luke spluttered, rushing at his friend and groping for the hose.

Tom had been playing jokes on him all weekend: dead mice in his workboots, a broken chair leg strategically concealed. It was about time Luke got his own back.

He fought Tom for the hose, knocking him to the ground and shoving his fingers up into his armpits so hard that Tom squealed like a girl and let go. The hose snaked wildly, twisting in the air and sending arcs of water from one end of the yard to the other. A jet slashed across Lawson's chest as he walked out of the shed to see what the commotion was. A look of thunder crossed his face.

'Now you've done it.' Luke pinned Tom's arms down into the mud. 'Lawson's gonna get you *bad*.' He let go of Tom and stepped aside as Lawson, bigger than the two of them put together, stormed towards them.

'He's all yours,' grinned Luke. Tom squirmed in a pool of mud and looked sheepishly at Lawson.

'Get that hose turned off and stop wasting water, Tom. You oughta know better than that.'

'Sorry, Lawson,' said Tom, struggling to keep a straight face.

Luke grabbed for the wayward hose and kinked it while Tom pulled himself up and walked towards the tap. Luke followed, and as soon as it was tightly shut off he made a grab for the designer undies peeping out the top of Tom's jeans and gave his mate the biggest, hardest wedgie he could. 'Take that back to boarding school with you,' he laughed, and bolted for the stables, leaving Tom cursing and clutching the back of his jeans.

Harry was in the stable aisle. Luke stopped in his tracks, dripping wet, and stared at him. Harry: the big charismatic man with the twinkling blue eyes, wheezy cough and leathery skin. He looked so frail and colourless.

'Hi, Harry,' Luke said, shaking his arms off.

'How'd you go with the hay?' The old man fumbled in

his pockets and brought out a pouch of tobacco.

'All stacked,' said Luke.

'Any good?'

'Nice and fresh, leafy. It's good.'

'Find that loose stallion?'

Luke startled. 'I thought . . .' He looked over Harry's shoulder. Biyanga stood in his stable, chewing on a mouthful of hay.

Harry chuckled. 'Tom got you a beauty.'

Luke watched Tom walk into the building, still pulling at his backside. 'I got him better.'

'You nearly cut me in half,' grumbled Tom, as he walked to the feedroom. 'Feeding up?'

Luke pulled the ute keys out of his pocket and jangled them. 'Sunday, they all get hay!' He looked hopefully at the old man, who stood there hand-rolling a ciggie. 'Gonna come, Harry?'

Harry slowly ran his tongue along the edge of the cigarette paper and then rolled it shut between his fingers and thumbs. He shrugged. 'Yeah, Annie'll kill me if she sees me smoking this thing.'

Luke's heart leapt. Harry hadn't been down to the paddock for over a week. He must be feeling a lot better. Luke walked over to the old man and took him gently by the arm.

Harry shook him off. 'No need for that,' he grumbled and shuffled towards the ute, taking big, laboured breaths. 'You drive.'

Luke ran to yank the door open for him, then jumped into the driver's seat. 'You're in the back, Tom!'

Tom came out of the feedroom looking sharp in a fresh change of city clothes. 'Can't,' he said, slinging a pack over his shoulder. 'Dad's here.' A horn honked out the front of the property. 'See you in a few weeks, ay?'

Luke slumped. It had been good having Tom around for the weekend. 'Thanks for the help with the hay,' he said, closing the door and winding the window down.

'Look after my horse for me!' Tom ran to the gate.

Luke waved out the window and then glanced at Harry, who was lighting up – unbelievable. Luke crunched the ute into gear, pumped the accelerator, then hung his head and half his body out the window while reversing to the top of the laneway. After opening the gate, he kept reversing, all the way down.

At the bottom he pulled his head back into the cabin. Harry stared at him with a puzzled expression.

'Something with the crankshaft,' shrugged Luke. 'Lawson's gonna look at it this week.' He yanked on the handbrake.

Harry raised an eyebrow, then dragged in a lungful of

smoke, wheezing and spluttering as he exhaled.

Luke tried not to listen to it. How a man with lung cancer could keep sucking on those things was beyond him. 'I tightened up all those fences, replaced two of the posts,' he said, pointing to the other side of the mares' paddock. 'They came up real good. And I fixed the ball-cock in the trough. It runs heaps better now.'

Harry kept coughing. Luke walked to the back of the ute and grabbed a whole bale of hay. He'd show Harry the cut on that filly's leg once he got them all fed. It wasn't healing right. Out in the paddock, he spread the bale out between the horses, then headed back for another one.

Harry was slumped over in the front of the ute with his eyes closed.

'Oh no, Harry.' Luke broke into a run, leapt the fence in a bound and yanked the door open. In the front seat, Harry took long squeaky pulls for air. The ciggie smouldered quietly, burning into his trousers. Luke grabbed it and flicked it out of the car. 'You okay, Harry?'

Harry didn't respond.

Luke gave him a gentle shake. 'Harry?'

The old man squeezed his eyes shut and sucked harder for air.

Luke slammed the door and ran to the driver's side. He crunched and crunched at the gears, but couldn't get it into first. 'Hang in there, Harry.' He pressed the horn on the steering wheel and a limp whine came out. Leaping out and dragging the gate open, he yelled '*Lawson!*' as loud as he could. 'Hold on, Harry!'

Luke reversed at full speed into the mares' paddock, scattering the horses, then hit the brakes and sent the ute into a one-eighty. He reversed back out, not bothering with the gate and flew backwards straight up the laneway, bumping and banging the whole way. Harry slumped onto the dashboard, fighting for breath.

He yelled for Lawson again as he entered the stable yard. Lawson came running. He opened Harry's door and immediately reached into his pocket for his phone.

'He can't breathe!' said Luke, as he leaned across and helped Harry to sit back. The old man's eyes were wide open and his neck strained. 'He's not getting any air in at all!'

While Lawson gave the nearest crossroad to the triple-0 service, Annie ran up behind him. She pulled him out of the way and knelt down by Harry. 'What've you done to yourself, love?' she said gently, holding her husband up. She looked across at Luke. 'Was he sneaking fags again?'

Luke froze. He didn't want to dob on the old man.

'Was he or not?' snapped Annie.

Luke nodded.

Annie set her lips tight and shook her head. 'You've got lung cancer, you old fool!' She pulled a puffer from her pocket and tried to squirt it into Harry's mouth. 'Try to breathe in, love.' She turned to Lawson. 'How long till they get here?'

'Twenty minutes.'

'He won't last twenty minutes!' Annie began frantically squeezing the inhaler at Harry's lips. 'Come on, love, *breathe*.'

'Help me sit him up,' said Lawson. Luke reached across the ute and helped to hold the old man up.

'Don't you give up, Harry!' said Lawson. 'Keep trying. Get that air in.'

Harry lifted his head and sucked for air.

'That's it, relax your shoulders, stay calm,' said Lawson. 'Keep trying, the ambulance is coming, you just gotta keep sucking in what air you can, old man.'

MOONSTONE PROMISE

Jess untied something from around her neck and held it
out to Luke. 'Take my moonstone. They're supposed to give
you beautiful dreams.'
It was a pale oval-shaped stone, hung on a thin leather strap.
'Promise me you'll come back,' she whispered.
'I'll see you again, Jess,' Luke said. 'Promise.'

After a harsh childhood spent in foster care, Luke finally feels
at home on Harry's farm, working with horses. When Harry dies,
and Luke has a bitter falling-out with the people around him,
he does a runner, leaving everything behind. He takes off to the
gulf country in search of brumbies and finds himself camped
by a river with three Aboriginal elders.

Can a mob of wild brumbies and three wise men help
Luke discover who he is and where he belongs?

OPAL DREAMING

*'What did you decide to call her?' asked Lawson,
looking over Jess's shoulder at the little chestnut foal.
'Opal,' said Jess, gazing, besotted, at her once-in-a-lifetime horse.
'Bad luck stones,' grunted Lawson.*

Finally the day has come when Jess can bring home her filly Opal.
But after Opal almost drowns in a flooded river, she becomes ill
and won't get better.

When Opal becomes so savage with pain that no one can
go near her, Jess wonders if the secrets of the land might hold
a cure, and jumps at the chance to go droving with her
friends – and Luke.

Can Jess find the answers she's seeking – and her dream boy
as well?